John Mark

A Gospel Novel

JOHN MARK

A Gospel Novel

by Christopher Epting

Ken —
Blessings + Peace!

RED MOON PUBLICATIONS
Oklahoma City, OK 73120

Cover Art and Illustrations by Suzanne Charleston,
www.suzanneartist.com

Book Layout by Lana B. Callahan, www.lbsdesignstudio.com

Library of Congress Control Number: 2012950423
ISBN 978-0-9851419-1-2

Printed in the United States of America

ACKNOWLEDGMENTS

My deepest thanks are offered to those who have made the writing of this little book possible:

To the Episcopal Diocese of Iowa for the generous sabbatical policy which has provided the time and space to produce this extended meditation;

To my dedicated staff for handling things so smoothly in my absence;

To St. George's College in Jerusalem for the "Desert Course" and "The Palestine of Jesus" both of which contributed so much to the context;

To my family for their constant love and encouragement;

And finally to my gifted assistant Julianne Allaway for producing the manuscript in the midst of her many other responsibilities...

God bless you all.

INTRODUCTION

This is an extended meditation--verse by verse, chapter by chapter--on the earliest Christian Gospel ever written, The Gospel of Mark. I began it years ago following a wonderful sabbatical, part of which was spent at St. George's College in Jerusalem and have worked on it, off and on, ever since.

I began each day with an early morning reflection/ meditation on some verses and chapters of this fast-moving account of Jesus' life and ministry and then attempted to tell the story as though "you were there" through the eyes of its presumed author, a man named John Mark. I have tried to incorporate my experience of traveling in and around the Palestine of Jesus, hopefully bringing to life some of those places and events referred to in the Gospel itself.

I have also tried to incorporate, to the best of my ability, the insights contemporary New Testament scholarship brings to the text without in any way changing or simply "explaining away" the events recounted or changing any basic elements of the story as Mark originally recounted it. I have sought to set the stage for Mark's understanding of the purpose of his Gospel in a brief "Prologue" and, after concluding the story (as I believe he did) with "the shorter ending," I have tried to supplement the two "longer endings" in the "Epilogue" with what tradition tells us of Mark's life after completing his work on the Gospel.

Whether I have been successful in any of this will, of course, depend upon the readers' analysis. I know that the very exercise itself has been a blessing to me…as I hope it may be to others.

PROLOGUE

My name is John Mark and this is a different kind of book. I suppose all authors believe that about their work even if they do not say it. But I want to be clear from the outset that my intention is to do more than tell a story. It is to introduce you to a person--he who is the central character of this book.

And it is he rather than the events of the story itself who has caused it to be written. I write these words years after the events they describe. So perhaps I may be forgiven if some of the details are sketchy.

What I hope will not be sketchy is the impact of the man about whom I write.

CHAPTER ONE

John might well have stayed with the teacher of righteousness and his brothers at Qumran had it not been for one basic disagreement. Although he had followed their progression from fire to water, from animal sacrifice to ritual purification, John wanted that message to reach the masses while his brothers were more interested in preparing themselves for their rapidly approaching judgment. So John left the community and struck out on his own into the bleak Judean wilderness.

I never knew if he consciously identified himself with Elijah or Isaiah or any of the old prophets, but it was pretty clear that the people did. It was amazing to me that people would walk for hours in the blazing sun to sit at his feet on the bank of the Jordan in order to be told that they must turn their lives completely around. The message certainly did not have an immediate appeal to me. I had no interest in those days whatsoever in naming my personal sins and shortcomings for all to hear and undergoing some ritual washing which was supposed to assure me of God's forgiveness and symbolize my willingness to lead a new kind of life. I was relatively satisfied with my life as it was.

I was impressed with John though. He was rough-hewn and a man of the desert, a bit hard to take for someone with my urban sensibilities. But there was a fire in him which made him somehow compelling. This was all the more fascinating to me because John's message did not revolve around himself or what he was going to do for the people. We were hearing a lot of that kind of thing in those days. Instead, John kept pointing beyond himself to "one who was coming," to one even more gifted, to one whose sandals he was unworthy to untie. And as important as John believed his baptism to be, this coming one would baptize with God's very own spirit. Now that got my attention! To be baptized, inundated, with the same spirit as the kings and prophets of old. It was for that my soul was longing...even if I was only beginning to recognize it.

It must have been about that time--at the height of John's ministry--that Jesus decided to undergo this baptism of repentance. He had, of course, grown up in the small town of Nazareth up in the Galilee, that lovely fertile region in the north. He must have heard something of John's message and was as attracted to him as so many others had been. When the invitation was given by the Baptist, Jesus apparently joined the crowds in wading into the little river. Down he went under the tepid water just like the scores of others John immersed that day. Just another penitent, just another observant Jew who wanted something more. Not just a good life (like mine). A new life. A life with meaning

And, to hear him tell the story years later, that is exactly what happened. As the waters of the Jordan closed in over his face, he felt that part of him was dying and being buried forever. Forever left behind him, drowned in that green water. But as John brought him up through the river's surface it was as if the waters above the firmament, as well as the waters below, were torn apart. It was as if that spirit which had once swept over the face of the primal waters now resided upon and within him. From deep within him, or from somewhere far away, he sensed a kinship, a oneness with the source of that spirit, the kind of convergence which says, "You are part of all this...you are one with all this ...you have a special role to play in all this. You are precious. You are mine."

The experience became formative for Jesus but not immediately. What he felt immediately was a rush of conflicting emotions, and what he saw ahead of him was a myriad of different paths. The sense of being part of a greater whole, the sense of being called by God, the sense of being simultaneously loved by and filled with God was clear. But how exactly was that to be lived out? What kind of life was he to live? More importantly, what kind of person was he to be? These were questions he could not yet answer and yet they were questions which had to be answered. And answered soon.

So, like Moses and Elijah before him, like the brothers of Qumran and their disciples, like men and women from all the ages have done and, I suppose, will continue to do, Jesus went into the desert. In his case, the desert was the Judean wilderness. Mile after mile of rocky, sun baked hills, the desert is an inhospitable and an unforgiving place taken on its own. A man can die in less than half a day if he is without water and without shade. And one unfamiliar with the terrain can become hopelessly lost in just an hour's walk outside a major city like Jerusalem.

And yet in spite of all this, indeed because of all this, the desert is a place of encounter. It is a place to meet and wrestle (like our ancestor) with God and with the demons. For, apart from the effort it takes to survive, there are no distractions in the desert. When one is alone there, the silence is profound and the images and concepts with which one must deal arise from within. The choices are simple, if not easy. Life or death, obedience or rebellion, God or Satan. All these Jesus confronted, day after solitary day, in the harsh desert country of Judea.

He saw relatively few signs of life, save his own, during

John Mark

"...the desert is a place of encounter..."

those days and weeks. Ants, a serpent, the occasional bird, foxes mewing in the night, and once a lion out, for some reason, early in the evening. But he was not alone in the desert. For there are gentle and hospitable spirits who make the desert their home as well. They know how tenuous life can be in that environment. And they keep watch for strangers and sojourners. So the one who came to serve had to learn first to be served.

About that time, Herod arrested John. I can still feel the tremor that shook our community upon hearing the news. It was on the lips of everyone--men who gathered to discuss the day's events under the shade of a tent, women drawing water from the well, even young people in their natural gathering places. It seemed for a time that this might touch off the revolt for which the zealots among us were constantly hoping and which truly always seemed to be bubbling just under the surface of daily events. But we were too weak and too frightened of Roman might seriously to entertain that notion. So, after a few days, the fury and excitement died down and the topic of John's arrest began to be discussed with a kind of grudging resignation and with much shaking of heads. Later, it would turn into a kind of corporate depression.

Suddenly, and without any warning, Jesus returned to his native Galilee! He had been away for some time and no one knew exactly why. Some said that he had had a falling out with his family, others that he had joined the Qumran community after his baptism by John, still others that he was engaged in a period of preparation and study on his own. All I know is that, when he returned, he looked lean and hard, darker of skin and steadier of gaze than when he left.

There seemed to be a new energy and new source of enthusiasm as well. He and his family had always been faithful and observant Jews, regular in attendance at the Nazarene synagogue and generally scrupulous in Sabbath and holy day obligations. But they were a quiet family and, after Joseph's death, had become even more quiet and reserved. But this new Jesus sounded like a prophet! He spoke of God in a deeply personal way and was able to generate the kind of excitement in a crowd that I had only seen before in someone like John the Baptist. They hung on every word and came away feeling encouraged and renewed in their faith and happy about being descendents of Abraham, Isaac, and Jacob.

The difference between Jesus' message and John's was interesting. John was always anticipating the future, looking forward to a time when God would act decisively in history and the coming one would baptize with the Holy Spirit. Jesus was saying that the time had arrived! "God's governance is not to be found in some future age," he would often shout,

"It is at hand for those with eyes to see and ears to hear!" He challenged people to turn around and embrace this new understanding, to trust that this wonderful message was true.

And gradually people in and around the Sea of Galilee began to do just that. Jesus loved the Galilee, and he loved the Sea of Galilee. The blue waters of this inland lake seemed to have a calming effect on him and he would walk for hours along its shores. Thus it was only natural for him to make the acquaintance of others who derived their sustenance from this important body of water in northern Palestine. Jesus seemed especially attracted to the fishermen. And the feeling was mutual. They were plain spoken men who, like farmers, knew that they were dependent upon the creator and the creation with its natural cycles for their particular kind of harvest. Adequate snow and rainfall during the winter meant high water and an abundant supply of fish. Drought conditions meant higher levels of salt in the water and a subsequent lowering of numbers fish in the Sea of Galilee.

The fishermen liked Jesus, first of all, because he listened to them. He seemed genuinely interested in their work and, when he asked questions, they could tell that he was really wanted to know the answer and was not just humoring them. So, Jesus' affinity for the fishing community of the Galilee was well known and I do not think it surprised any of us when, one afternoon at the end of a particularly discouraging day of fishing, Jesus invited two brothers--Andrew and Simon--to leave it all behind and to follow him. I think we were all waiting for some kind of community to form around Jesus. His message was certainly compelling and was beginning to attract a fairly wide following of people like myself who, while not willing yet to commit ourselves, did not want to be too far away from him lest we miss something of significance for ourselves and for our history.

Besides, John and a number of others like him had established small communities of disciples. Why should Jesus be any different? So it was no surprise that Jesus' new friends, Simon and Andrew, responded favorably to his call. They had had a relationship with him already. But no one I knew expected James and John, those boisterous and thoroughly secular sons of Zebedee to join the new community. First of all, they were unlikely candidates personally. And secondly, their father needed them badly in his fishing business. It was one of the larger operations in the Galilee and Zebedee needed all the help he could get. As I look back on it now, it is no wonder that Jesus came under a good bit of criticism for the impact his call for radical discipleship had on families. It may have all started with James and John.

Be that as it may, Jesus and his small community began to travel along the northern coast of the Sea of Galilee and soon found themselves in Capernaum, one of the more prosperous cities of the day. Since it was Friday and the Sabbath was fast approaching, they located the synagogue and began to anticipate the weekly day of rest, study, and worship which was really the holiest day of them all for our people.

Like most synagogues, the one in Capernaum provided not only a place to worship the God of Israel, but a gathering place for various rabbis and teachers and their students to study Torah, discuss various interpretations of the texts, and seek a deeper understanding of God's ways through the process of rabbinical dialogue, debate, and even argument. Jesus was a master of this kind of study and genuinely seemed to look forward to raising the particularly thorny issues arising from the biblical text. He had apparently attracted quite a crowd on this day because of his willingness to bring up new ideas and to speak out his bold insights and interpretations with a kind of fresh passion rather than to rehash some of the same tired old arguments people were accustomed to hearing from the scribes.

Synagogues were, of course, available by right to all Jewish males on the Sabbath and, like places of worship in all religious traditions, attracted all sorts and conditions of people--solid citizens of the community, farmers, merchants, poor people, nomadic folks, and almost invariably, a small percentage of those who could only be described as fanatics.

These last were wild-eyed, self-styled prophets who had little or no credibility or following but who would, at the slightest opportunity, proceed to expound their own rather bizarre version of the law or the prophets.

The members of the Capernaum synagogue community had always thought that this particular individual fell into the latter category and had tended to be somewhat tolerant of him. He was something of an embarrassment, but the rabbis could normally keep him under control and from dominating the discussion and so ruining the day for everyone.

No so on this particular occasion. Wandering as always from group to group, rabbi to rabbi, this man became fixated on Jesus and on what he was saying. He became increasingly agitated and finally blurted out something about Jesus not fitting in and how he was going to destroy Judaism with this kind of talk. But then, strangely, he said that he recognized Jesus as a holy one sent by God!

This breach of etiquette was unacceptable as was the blasphemous suggestion that one sent by God was undermining the faith that same God had given to the Jews. The man was clearly beside himself and completely deluded into supposing that God's messenger was attacking the things of God. Jesus spoke to him firmly like he was a naughty child and the man seemed to fulfill that very role by throwing himself on the floor sobbing and screaming in rage, frustration, and embarrassment. It appeared to many as if there were some kind of spiritual or emotional purging process going on. Finally, utterly exhausted, the man lay still, breathing heavily.

From the shocked silence of the synagogue community, gradually a few quiet murmurings grew into a noisy buzz of speculation about what had just happened and about the events leading up to it and about the principle players, particularly Jesus. Most felt that he had handled a difficult situation well and had taken charge when even the local rabbis seemed unsure what to do. They were also impressed with the fact that Jesus' words seemed to have an observable effect on people. When he taught certainly, but even on this most troubled among them--the man who had confronted Jesus.

Indeed it was the fact that Jesus' words and actions where so consistent and so intertwined that began to make him well known in the Galilee. His practice and his proclamation were one. That was evident to even the most casual observer. And that quality is so rare. The quality is called integrity and I think somehow it is at the core of what came to be known as Jesus' healing ministry. His message was one of the sovereignty and goodness of God and it was so compelling and right that when it came up against sickness or suffering of any kind, that sickness and suffering simply could not stand.

Take the example of Simon's mother-in-law. Right after the dramatic events in the Capernaum synagogue, the five of them decided to spend the night with the family of Simon and Andrew. James and John were not in the best favor with their parents and were not at this time, even welcome in their own home. But Simon's family was always somehow easier with the strange choice he had made and encouraged him pretty much to come and go as he willed.

That evening, just as they entered, Simon's wife informed him that her mother was ill. She had had a fever for several days and had been unable to rise from her bed without feeling dizzy and faint. Simon initially informed Jesus of the situation, not expecting him to do anything about it, but by way of apology that the food would be a little late in coming. Jesus asked if he might see her and they led him into one of the rooms toward the rear of the house. He squatted down beside her pallet, resting comfortably on his heels, and grasped her hand. Andrew later told me that they engaged in some quiet conversation for ten or fifteen minutes. Before he could even think of what to say, he saw his brother's mother-in-law rise up from her bed, assisted by Jesus, and join her daughter in preparing food for their guests. Her illness, whatever it was, was no match for the concern she felt from Jesus about her health and well-being.

As you can imagine, the combination of the morning's

excitement at the synagogue and the rapidly spreading news about Simon's mother-in-law and her unexpected recovery attracted quite a bit of attention in this particular neighborhood of Capernaum. In fact, as soon as the sun began to set and the Sabbath was ended, a crowd began to gather in front of the home of Andrew, Simon, and their families. There were even people there from across town and it seemed that everyone had with them a friend or a relative who was suffering from some kind of physical, spiritual, or emotional distress.

Jesus looked on these with compassion and concern. He asked his four friends to usher the sick folks in one and a time so that he could speak and pray with them. Many left feeling whole and restored. As had been the case that morning in the synagogue, some of these were deranged and tormented souls who were less than cooperative with Jesus and his assistants. Simon said that Jesus used the same stern tone of voice with these as he had with the man in the synagogue. Not that it was a voice devoid of compassion. It was more that Jesus was able to make a distinction between the person and the force or forces which were destroying the person. To the person Jesus spoke warmly, to the destructive power, even if it manifested itself through the person, Jesus spoke sternly and directly.

Occasionally, these latter would seek to debate Jesus or

engage him in further conversation once the healing was accomplished. He would have none of it, nor of owning the various laudatory titles and praises which many attempted to lavish upon him. He rarely permitted further conversation. James thought that was simply because it was now well into the night and more awaited Jesus' attention. John thought there was another reason, and it was that recurring quality of Jesus not wanting to take credit for the healing. He knew who he was. And he was more than a worker of wonders.

In order to keep that sense of perspective, Jesus needed a certain amount of silence and solitude. On this very occasion, even though the last supplicants had not disappeared from Simon's entryway until very late, when his friends rose at daybreak, Jesus' bed was empty and he was nowhere to be found in and around the house. When Simon and the others did find him, it was a great ways out in the country, atop a small hill. At first they were surprised that he did not seem to notice their approach or acknowledge them at all. But when he rose, they realized that he had been praying. His face was serene and he seemed deeply rested even though they knew that he could only have gotten a few hours' sleep. It would often be that way for him after he prayed. The deep communion he experienced with his God brought renewal and refreshment in a way that mere sleep never did.

His friends were somewhat annoyed at him for not having

told them where he was going so early in the day. They informed him that the whole household was looking for him and had been concerned, but he ignored their implied criticism, knowing that they would soon learn his patterns and his ways and suggested that they move on to Chorazin. Acchabare, and Sepph, the next Galilean towns he had planned to visit. There was a certain resignation in his voice which suggested that, if he had his way, he might have remained there all day to pray. But he knew that his mission was to reach others with the message of God's reign and God's love, and that everything else must be subservient to that.

The next weeks were filled with long early morning walks through the beautiful countryside of the Galilee: afternoons in which his friends would move about the towns inviting the local people to the synagogue or some other gathering place to hear Jesus teach in the evenings. His reputation as one who could bring healing to body, mind, and spirit had preceded him and it was the rare gathering that did not result in numerous people presenting themselves for healing prayer, and returning to their homes free of whatever had been assaulting them.

Even lepers, and others with disfiguring skin diseases, felt able to present themselves before this man of compassion and integrity. Normally, of course, they stayed well out of the mainstream of daily life. Some had to wear bells or otherwise make their presence known so that people could get out of their way. There was such fear on most people's part that they would either catch the disease or somehow become contaminated or affected by whatever heinous sin the leper must have committed to have been so stricken. And so it was that a particular individual in Accabare approached Jesus very gingerly and tentatively, "If you will, sir, you can make me clean."

"If I will," Jesus replied with the pain of all that that man had experienced in his voice. "Of course I will!" And rather than simply praying for him at a distance as he did with some people, it seemed that Jesus made a special point of laying his hands upon him, full upon the repulsive, open sores as he declared, rather than prayed, "Be clean!" And the man was cured. Well, you can imagine the gasp and roar of the crowd who witnessed this. Yet Jesus seemed annoyed by that and, rather than basking in the moment or even rejoicing with them and with the man, Jesus touched him once again. This time, almost roughly, by the shoulder he held him and spoke with urgency in his voice, "Do not say anything to anyone about this! God is the healer here, not me. Now do what Moses commanded us in the law for this kind of thing. Go show yourself to a priest so that he can verify the validity of the cure and make an offering to God as an expression of the fact that you know where this came from."

Of course, Jesus might as well have told the man to stop breathing as to keep the news of his healing from his family and his friends and all those who had known him before and would see him cleansed and whole. He could not possibly keep it to himself, and perhaps Jesus knew that. His warning did serve to help people remember that, in this sense, he was like John the Baptist--always pointing beyond himself, in his case not to one who would come, but to the One from whom all good things come.

The fact that the man cured from his skin disease was unable to keep quiet about it all (as were most of the rest of us, frankly, who had seen it all occur) did mean that our itinerary had to be altered significantly. For the next several weeks it was simply impossible for us to visit the cities and urban areas directly as he had hoped. The crowds too quickly became mobs and the clamoring for healing or for other wonders precluded anyone from hearing Jesus teach. This was a great disappointment to him, but we finally convinced him to remain in the open country while we assembled smaller, but more attentive gatherings made up mostly of those we knew had an interest in learning more of God's truth, not just seeing more of God's power.

CHAPTER TWO

After a few days, we decided to risk a return to his home in Capernaum. We actually had a few quiet hours to ourselves before the word began to circulate through the community that he was back. Before we knew it, the little home they had purchased after Joseph's death and their move from Nazareth was overflowing with those who wanted to hear him teach as well as those who asked prayers for healing.

As always, Jesus spoke to them about the fact that God was in charge of their lives and of the world now and not just at some future date when God's sovereignty would be once and for all established. He seemed to be concerned that the hopes of his people for a future in-breaking of God's reign dimmed their eyes and stopped their ears from perceiving God's presence and direction in the world about them. Jesus' logic was convincing and his eloquence persuasive to many.

It was fortunate that his voice was strong and clear and could be heard at great distances--especially fortunate on this occasion because of a noisy clamor which arose toward the front of the house. I slipped outside and saw a group of fifteen or so surrounding a smaller group of four who were carrying a pallet upon which lay a man who appeared to be very ill. They tried to push their way through the crowded doorway, but those who had gotten there ahead of them would have none it.

It used to bother me that those who came seeking the gift of healing for themselves were so often the first to deny it to others. I suppose it has something to do with the desperation of the seriously ill and the self-centered attitude they quite naturally develop in order to survive, not unlike babies who cry when they are hungry or wet. At any rate, the noise subsided a bit as the four fell back from the crowded front steps. I had thought that they might have given up hope of ever getting their friend to Jesus when suddenly I noticed dust and then a few sticks and other bits of roofing material falling into Jesus' hair and onto his shoulders. The four friends were removing a section of the roof, obviously in order to lower their friend to the feet of Jesus.

This caused an immediate outcry but Jesus silenced them with a gesture and smiled his encouragement to those on the roof. It was obvious that they believed Jesus could bring healing to their friend and that they would stop at nothing to see that he was given the chance. As the mat was lowered down to the floor, I saw why the sick man needed his friends' help. He could not have walked to Jesus on his own. He could not walk at all. Jesus knelt on one knee at the paralytic's side and began to speak to him about God's love and forgiveness. I found that he would nearly always do that, not because he believed that sickness is always the result of sin, but because much of the prevailing theology of the day had made that linkage and sick people were often tormented by the thought of what they must have done to have been punished so severely.

Jesus was about to continue speaking with the man when he was suddenly interrupted by the voice of one of the scribes who had been listening to him teach. "Do you hear what this man is saying? It is blasphemous. He doesn't even know what this man's sins are and yet he presumes to forgive them instead of leaving that to God's judgment?" Jesus raised his gaze to meet that of the scribe. He looked intently at the man for a few moments, seeking to discern whether or not this was a legitimate question for discussion or debate or simply an attempt to make him look foolish. He asked the man, "Why do you agonize over this question? Which should I have said first to this man, 'Your sins are forgiven'; or 'Rise, take up your bed and walk'?"

The scribe was about to attempt an answer when Jesus did his own interrupting. He said to the scribe, "Just so that you will know that I have power on earth to forgive sins," and then he turned to the paralytic, "Rise, take up your bed, and go home." And slowly, on shaky knees and with muscles long unused, the man got up, folded his pallet, and gazed gratefully and tearfully into the eyes of Jesus for nearly a full minute before making his way through the hushed crowd as it melted away before his new-found steps.

Even with the healings we had witnessed earlier, this was more than we had anticipated. The crowd was ecstatic and I had to agree that I had never seen anything like it. I resolved then and there to stay close to this itinerant rabbi for surely God was doing something new through him. I was not the only one to be so convinced for, as we moved out from the city, seeking again the cool breezes of the Sea of Galilee, Jesus caught sight of an old friend who name was Levi.

Now Levi was hardly the most popular figure in Capernaum. In fact he was roundly hated by his Jewish fellows because he had sold out to the occupying forces and made a pretty decent living exacting tax and toll from his own people. And he was equally disliked by the Romans because he was either none too good at this job, or he was letting some people off too easily because his revenues were always short. But Jesus had always loved the little tax collector.

He knew that Levi detested his life and had, on more than one occasion, challenged him to leave it, to make a new start.

Always before, Levi would listen carefully, then drop his eyes, shake his head, and start to make excuses as to why he needed to stay. But that was before the healing of the paralytic; that was before Jesus'exchange with the scribe and his conviction about the forgiveness of sins. Maybe there was hope. Maybe new beginnings were possible. So this time, when Jesus said, "Why don't you follow me?" Levi followed. And, from that day, he called himself by a new name to symbolize the gift of his new life--Matthew, the gift from God.

Later, we were all having a dinner of fish, bread, olives, and melon at Matthew's house. It was a strange assortment of people that evening as I look back on it. Other tax gatherers who were friends and associates of Matthew, poor people who never paid any taxes anyway, a few thieves who should have paid but never did, women (some of whom were devoutly religious and some of whom were decidedly not), several of Jesus' inner circle, and a number of hangers-on like me. Quite a conglomeration. But then Matthew could not be too discriminating about his friends, and Jesus simply never had been. He seemed to move easily between the richest and poorest people in town, between the most religious and the least, between Jew and Gentile.

This prompted a question from one of Matthew's guests, who happened to be one of the Pharisee's scribes. He leaned over to Andrew and asked, "Why does your teacher eat and drink with these kinds of people?" The scribe, of course, had seen to it that he had eaten something before he came to Matthew's house, knowing the type of company he would be keeping, and he reclined conspicuously back from the table to make sure everyone was aware of that fact. Andrew, however, had just taken a big mouthful of food and, before he could chew it, swallow, and answer, Jesus answered for him, having overheard the question from across the table.

"How many hale and hearty people--people like yourself, Joah--did you see flocking to my door earlier today? Not many. Because those who are in that category have no need of a doctor. Those who are sick have that need. My message is not intended for those who are right with God. It is intended for those who are not." With that, Jesus returned to his meal leaving Joah the scribe, and the rest of us to wonder, Were we "right with God" or were we not?

Not many days after this, we came into a season of fasting and penitence. Almost everyone, from the most liberal of the Pharisees to those still fiercely dedicated to the imprisoned John the Baptist, was participating in the fast. Jesus had simply never mentioned it to us and it was obvious from his own behavior that he had no intention whatsoever of observing this particular fast. Like his lack of good judgment in choosing table companions, this was bound to raise questions on the part of some.

This time, however, even the common people were puzzled. Fasting was widely observed during this time and it seemed out of character for a normally observant Jew like Jesus to refuse to participate. Some asked him about it and he answered by citing a line or two from Isaiah which did not immediately appear to bear upon the question.

Seeing our confusion, he smiled and said, "Fasting is not appropriate at a wedding feast, is it? How would it look for the guests to say that they were fasting while the bride and groom are celebrating their marriage? But have no fear, wedding banquets do not last forever. There will be plenty of time to fast." "Are you saying then," John asked him, "that we no longer need to observe the traditions of our ancestors now that you are with us?"

"I'm saying that it does no good to try and patch an old coat with new cloth. It doesn't match. It doesn't work," Jesus replied, "Any more than it works to pour fresh new wine into an old, dried-out container. The container will simply burst. It cannot hold the new wine and, if we try to make it, the new wine will be lost. So then, new wine requires a new container!"

It was only then that many of us began to realize just how revolutionary Jesus' message was. He did not intend merely to reform Judaism. He intended to transform it. Nowhere was this more clearly seen than in the way Jesus dealt with Shabbat, with the Sabbath day. Clearly he cherished the concept of Shabbat, regular periods of withdrawal from one's worldly activities for a time of rest, prayer, and study. Indeed Jesus' daily, weekly, and seasonal patterns provided for just such a rhythm between time to work and time to play, time to serve and time to pray.

What he could not abide was for rules and regulations concerning the Sabbath--many of which had no basis in the Torah--to be cited as excuses for failing to meet human need. For example, one Shabbat when we were actually on our way to the synagogue in Gamla, as we passed through a wheat field and discovered that we were hungry, several of us plucked off heads of grain, rubbed them between our hands, and nibbled on them for some refreshment.

Finishing as we climbed the little hill to enter the synagogue, we were immediately confronted by members of the Pharisees' party who accused us of breaking Shabbat. Jesus responded by telling them a story from the tradition about David. It appears that once this greatest of all our leaders had asked the high priest of that time for five loaves of bread for some men with whom he had an appointment. Finding himself short of those loaves, the high priest himself offered David some of the bread of the Presence which he took for the men, having assured the priest that--while they were not priests--the young men were pure and holy.

Actually, in his zeal to relate the story, Jesus identified the high priest in question as Abiathar when he later remembered it to be Ahimelech. But the Pharisees were so taken aback by Jesus' final comment that they did not even challenge him on the momentary lapse. For Jesus concluded his story with an astounding statement and claim. He said, "Shabbat was made for people, not people for Shabbat. So in that sense I am lord even of the Sabbath!" Of course, having said that, in the face of their stunned silence, Jesus led us immediately past the stone containers of water for ritual purification and into the little synagogue for Sabbath services. Several people had arrived early, among them one with a poorly formed right hand. I think we all knew what was going to happen. The tension in the room was as thick as the waters of the great salt sea. Jesus felt the eyes of the Pharisees on him, daring him to do what he knew he had to do. "Come here," he said to the man with the withered hand. And then, whirling on the Pharisees with his eyes flashing, he snapped, "Then just what is it lawful to do on the Sabbath? May we do good? Or are we only permitted to do harm? Should we save life if we can? Or kill?"

Well, they simply did not know how to answer. They knew that he had bested them (for there was only one godly answer to his question) but they were too proud or too cowardly to admit it. I could see, from where I was standing, that Jesus was furious at them. Yet his fury was tempered with a deep sadness. It wasn't really their fault, I heard him thinking to himself. Someone had trapped them into believing this foolishness. How far the faith of our forebears had fallen! With weariness in his voice, Jesus turned back to the man with the deformity. “Stretch out your hand.”

I swear to you, my readers, that when the man brought his right hand forth from beneath his coat, it was a whole as the left. Jesus had answered the question about Shabbat at least for himself. For this master of the Sabbath, it was always lawful to do good. The Pharisees walked out. And headed for Herod’s palace.

CHAPTER THREE

Concerned that these conflict situations might attract the attention of Herod or of the Roman authorities, Jesus led us back westward toward the Sea of Galilee. However, if he thought to avoid the crowds again and have some quiet time, he would have to think again. The crowds just seemed to get larger and larger. They came from as far south as Jerusalem in Judea and from as far north as Tyre in Phoenicia. How had they heard about him in so short a time?

Jesus told us to ready a small boat for him once it became clear that the crowd was pressing in upon him so as to make teaching impossible and the healing ministry difficult, even dangerous. For there seemed invariably to be numbers of persons with disturbed minds or spirits as well as those with broken and ravaged bodies. These would often become violent before completely reversing themselves and falling at Jesus' feet, lavishing praises and honors upon him. As in the synagogue at Capernaum, Jesus would always speak to them sternly and warn them to bridle their tongues concerning him and who they might believe him to be. For one of them had called him the son of God.

As it turned out, he did not have to escape by boat this time and the crowd gradually dissipated. Continuing our westward journey along the northern shore of the lake, we followed as he made his way to a mountain which overlooked the blue water. There must have been twenty or thirty of us but, as we came to the base of the mountain, he had us set up camp early while he moved among us speaking first to one and then to another. Just before evening fell, he led twelve of them up the mountain for an overnight together.

When they returned the next morning, we were told that these twelve would have special responsibilities from now on. They would spend somewhat more time with him alone, eventually would be sent out in pairs to proclaim God's reign just as Jesus was doing, and would even be given authority to pray for healing and for deliverance from the evil one in Jesus' name. In addition to the five he had already called personally, this inner circle included Philip from Bethsaida, Bartholomew (who I had always known as Nathanael), Thomas, James the son of Alphaeus, Thaddaeus (later Jude), Simon the Cananaean who was a member of the Zealot party, and Judas Iscariot another political revolutionary.

There was actually very little jealousy among the rest of us at these choices. Although it was an incredibly diverse and potentially volatile mixture of personalities and positions, each of the individuals chosen had one overriding characteristic--they were absolutely committed to the person and ministry of Jesus. Not that they all would have agreed on who or what he was. But they each loved him deeply and were fiercely loyal to him. None of the rest of us were yet that single-minded in our commitment to him. Curious, yes. Impressed, certainly. Willing to take the next step with him, surely. But we were not one with him yet. Not in the way that these twelve seemed to be. They became his family.

And it was good that they did because things were not going so well for Jesus at home. We found that out the next day when we returned to Capernaum. He tried to stay with his family, but discovered that they had had no peace since he left, so great were the crowds which began to assemble at daybreak each day and remained in small groups around the house until nightfall, hoping for his return.

Most of these people were, of course, supportive of Jesus and his message and were themselves seeking to learn more about him or the healing grace for which he had become known. But there was a contingent, mostly associated with the temple in Jerusalem, who were there to discredit Jesus and to sow seeds of doubt in the minds of any who would follow him. Their favorite technique was to accuse Jesus of worshipping Beelzebul, a pagan god who had become associated with the demonic, even with Satan himself.

Because Jesus' healing ministry had led him to interact with spiritual as well as physical sickness, there were some who had become fascinated with exorcism and wanted to elevate that to a special category rather than seeing it, as Jesus himself did, as the logical extension of the sovereignty of God when that sovereignty did not permit brokenness of body, mind, or spirit in the lives of people.

"He is possessed with Beelzebul," the scribes were saying to anyone in Capernaum who would listen. "It must be by this chief devil's own power that he had control over the other devils."

"Bring them to me." Jesus said. And a group of us dared them to confront Jesus with their charges to his face. They came with us and Jesus began to engage them in his favorite pastime, the give and take of rabbinic dialogue and debate.

Jesus: How can Satan cast out Satan?

Scribe: If Beelzebul is the prince of all demons, surely he can command them to come and go as he wills.

Jesus: But I am defeating and destroying the powers of evil not simply redirecting them. That would be like a king fighting his own troops! The kingdom would collapse. Or a family, torn by strife and enmity--it will not stand.

Scribe: Perhaps that is what is happening here. A war between devils.

Jesus: Satan divided? I don't see any signs of that or of any weakening of the demonic influence in this world. I wish I did. No, all I'm doing right now is acting like one who sneaks into a strong man's house at night to rob him. You have to tie him up first, while he's asleep, if you expect to steal his possessions.

But nothing would convince these particular opponents that Jesus' power was for good, not evil. He dismissed them with a warning: "I tell you solemnly, if you persist in this way of thinking, you are in mortal danger spiritually. The God I serve is gracious and full of compassion. There is virtually no sin --no matter how heinous--that God will not forgive if you ask and are open to receiving that forgiveness. But if you mistake the presence and power of God's spirit for that of a pagan god or even a devil, to whom would you turn for forgiveness? Your understanding of God and your values are so perverted, I'm not sure you would ever think to ask my God for forgiveness or be able to receive it properly if you did. How dare you accuse me of being led by an unclean spirit!"

After the scribes left, Jesus gathered us for a lengthy and passionate teaching on this whole matter. He reiterated that there were forces in this universe eternally opposed to the purposes of God, and reminded us of the importance of being grounded in the law and the prophets, of being faithful to prayer and meditation, of remaining true to the God of our ancestors and to each other in order to have the spiritual stamina necessary to carry on a demanding ministry such as the one to which he was calling at least some of us.

We were in the middle of this crucial point when a knock came at Simon's door, and Jesus was informed that his mother and brothers were outside, terribly upset because they had heard--probably from the same scribes--that he had lost his mind and was even following other gods.

"Is that what my family now believes of me?" Jesus asked in an angry voice. "Then from now on these are my mother and my brothers, the ones who understand me and seek to do God's will!" With these words, he indicated us. And I saw his mother's face fall as she realized that he no longer belonged in Capernaum. He was no longer one of them.

CHAPTER FOUR

Leaving the city once more, we made our way back to the sea shore. The boat we had secured for Jesus was still there and this time the crowd was sufficiently large and unruly that he decided to use it. He sat in the prow of the little vessel while Simon Peter (as Jesus now called him) and Andrew rowed out a little ways into the lake. At this particular spot, the hills slope directly down to the shore line and so the crowd was able to fan out up the side of the hill as well as along the beach, making a natural amphitheater. This configuration, coupled with Jesus' wonderful voice, allowed everyone to hear as he began to teach them, this time using parables for the first time.

He found that, while he had time with us to engage in the kind of dialogical teaching that he loved, that was simply not possible with large crowds. The question and answer style did not work because few people could hear the responses from members of the audience, and it was difficult to keep such a large crowd, with varied interests, on track. So Jesus began to use stories. Often these were familiar folk tales to which he gave a new twist. Sometimes the parables were original with him. Almost always, they were intended to make one simple point, to give people a glimpse (not an exhaustive analysis) of what God's reign was all about. He would say things like:

"Once a farmer scattered his seed broadcast. Naturally, some fell at his feet along the path where he walked only to be eaten quickly by the birds which followed him. Some fell on rocky ground barely covered with soil. Of course these sprang up within a few days, but they had no depth of soil in which to root so when the hot sun shone on them, they withered. Other seed feel among the thorns and weeds which choked the life from the young plant. But, even with all this unproductive seed, some landed in good soil and that seed produced a yield for the farmer of thirty, sixty, even a hundredfold. If you have ears to hear, then hear!"

We realized that he was explaining why it was that some people responded to his message so readily and some did not. There were a number of reasons--evil itself robbed the message of its power, people got discouraged over the long haul after initially embracing it, the desire for worldly success and acclaim strangle the life out of it. But, even with failure like that, some have ears to hear and they were the ones who bore fruit.

These he would challenge to stand with him and be visible advocates for the sovereignty of God over all things: "Do you light a lamp only to put it under a bushel basket? No, you put it on a stand so that it can give light to everyone! God's governance is not to be a secret. It is to be made known to everyone."

Sometimes the parables gave instructions for living: "Listen to me. The measure you give will be the measure you get!" At other times, they would be for the purpose of illustrating mysterious and difficult aspects of God's nature. "Of course we do not always understand how God's will is being played out in this world. We don't even understand exactly how the earth produces grain from the seed we sow! But that doesn't prevent us from putting in the sickle when the harvest comes, does it?"

"Yes, the signs that God really is in charge and is working his purposes out seem few now. But look at the size of a mustard seed when compared to the shrub it grows into. If you have ears, then hear." Many did, I think, because of the parables, while we continued our instruction with him well into every night around the camp fire.

Late one evening, he decided that we should cross the Sea of Galilee in order to enter the country of the Gergesenes in the tetrarchy of Philip. We often traveled at night to avoid the heat of day, but not usually when we went by boat.

John Mark

"He shouted so that we could hear him over the noise of the storm..."

Nonetheless, we sensed that he wanted to be there by morning so we arranged for several boats and launched out just as we were.

The lake is less than seven miles wide at that point, but a sudden gust of wind from the dry river beds which lead down to it can whip the normally tranquil surface of the sea into turmoil in a matter of minutes. That is exactly what happened! Before we knew it, we were in real trouble. The vessels were wrenched to and fro by the white capped waves and, more than once, the bows would dip beneath the water's surface, spilling gallons into the boats while we bailed furiously.

Jesus had been exhausted after a long day of teaching and had fallen asleep, shortly after we shoved off, in the stern of the largest boat on a cushion. We woke him as soon as the storm broke and alerted him to our situation...and to our fear! He shouted so that we could hear him over the noise of the storm, "Peace! Be still!" And before we knew it, the storm was over. It was as if even the wind and the sea obeyed him!

"Why were you so afraid?" he asked. "Don't you trust God to take care of us?" And with that he returned to the stern and fell at once to sleep.

After dropping anchor a short time later, we had to admit to one another that our faith had been shaken by the storm, but that it had certainly been strengthened by Jesus' response.

It was actually Matthew who remembered the words of the psalm:

"Then they cried to the Lord in their trouble, and he delivered them from their distress. He stilled the storm to a whisper and quieted the waves of the sea."

CHAPTER FIVE

When the sun was fully up we went ashore just north of Gergesa. Jesus had no sooner scrambled from the boat to the beach when an unbelievable figure--naked, filthy, and bleeding--came running toward us through the sand. We had heard of this man, whose name was Jeduthun, from visitors who had come to the Galilee from a federation of ten towns in this part of Palestine which the Romans called Decapolis.

Jeduthun had grown up just outside Gergesa and had been a burden to his family and to the community for many years. Always difficult to manage, never fitting in, he became increasingly difficult to deal with as he grew up. He would become physically violent the instant things did not go his way, and his parents had finally been forced by the neighbors to restrain him, first with rope and later even with a chain, so that people could feel at least somewhat safe with him in the area.

Being bound in this way only served to intensify the young

man's distress and he responded, with the almost superhuman strength of a madman, by breaking free of the rope and literally straightening the iron chain's clasp. After that, he refused to remain at home lest they tie him up again, and began to wander through the hill country, spending much of his time near the tombs even sleeping in one of the graves which had been desecrated by pagan vandals and later by animals much to the horror of the citizenry.

They would often hear him shrieking throughout the night from the agony of his tortured mind and spirit. His parents themselves were tormented by his tragic condition, their misery compounded by the fact that he had adopted the pagan practice of slashing and bruising himself with the sharp rocks which were everywhere. This seemed to everyone the outward manifestation of Jeduthun's misery and the self-loathing he so obviously felt. The whole situation was frightening and tragic.

Yet it was this man we saw shouting and stumbling his way closer and closer to Jesus. Peter, Andrew, James, and John quickly formed a kind of phalanx in front of Jesus to protect him from a physical assault. But Jesus stepped between them and shouted in the general direction of the approaching figure, "Come out of that man, you foul spirit!"

With that, Jeduthun pitched forward on his face in the sand and screamed through his tears and spittle, "What are you going to do to me, Jesus son of the Most High? I beg you in the name of God do not torture me!"

"What's your name?" Jesus asked, though I was sure he knew it was Jeduthun.

"My name? It must be Legion; for we are many. Please don't send us far away. Send us into the swine; they're as unclean as we are!"

"Then go!" Jesus said through clenched teeth, and the man roared with some unknown suffering we could not even imagine. The roar escalated into a blood-curdling howl and a large herd of pigs which had been peacefully grazing through all of this along a hillside bolted and began loping downhill toward the sea. Those in front stumbled down the steep incline and those behind became entangled in their hoofs and legs. Eventually, the whole lot ended up in the water, drowning before the herdsmen could do anything about it. I have never seen anything like it before or since!

Those who had been herding the pigs were most upset. They ran to Gergesa and to the surrounding countryside with the story and, before we knew it, we were surrounded with gawking onlookers wanting to know exactly what had happened. We did have time to revive Jeduthun, clean him up a bit, and get some clothes on him. He was, of course, exhausted and in shock but was able to eat and drink a little from our provisions, and seemed genuinely at peace for the first time in many, many years.

If the locals were impressed and appreciative because of what Jesus had just presided over, the swineherds were not. They had lost their entire livelihood in a matter of minutes and in a way they could not possibly explain to the owner. They wanted no part of Jesus and wished to see him no more, that day or any other. Finally, we persuaded him to change whatever plans he had for this Gergesene territory, and to get back into the boat before the crowd turned ugly, whipped up by the herdsmen. He reluctantly agreed and, as he was bidding farewell to Jeduthun, I heard the restored man ask him,

"Please let me go with you. I have no life here and perhaps I can be of some assistance to you as a way of paying you back for all you've done for me."

"No, Jeduthun," Jesus smiled, "Your work is here, among your own people. Show them that you are different, and tell them, not what I have done for you today, but what our God had done for you and healing grace is all about."

Jeduthun did exactly that, from what we heard. Not only in Gergesa, but in all the Ten Towns, he told his story, although he gave more credit to Jesus than our teacher would have wanted. Indeed Jesus' fame continued to spread across Palestine no matter how hard he tried to keep that from happening.

Sailing back across the lake, we put ashore near Taricheae only to be greeted there by a large crowd including a man named Jairus, whom Jesus knew because he was an important leader in the local synagogue. It was clear from the look on Jairus' face that he was more than upset. Frantic might be a better way to describe it. It did not take long for us to learn why as we saw Jairus kneel before Jesus and cry out: "Jesus, my little girl! She is sick, close to death they say. Come and lay your hands upon her, as you have on so many, that she may be made well and live!"

Jesus raised Jairus up and clasped him tightly by both shoulders. He gazed deeply into his eyes as if to impart some of his own strength and hope into the life of this distraught father. Jairus turned toward the little village where his daughter lay and Jesus followed without saying a word. It meant that he had to push his way through the crowd, many of whom had themselves needs for which they wanted him to pray. But Jesus seemed single-minded in his desire to reach Jairus' daughter before her situation deteriorated. The crowd fell in behind him in order to witness what might turn out to be another healing, and also to be near him so that when this visit was completed, he might turn his attention to them.

I saw him move past one women particularly pitiful in her weakness. The crowd was moving so rapidly and pressing in upon him so tightly that I doubt if he could have stopped to respond to this woman's plea even if he had been so minded. But, as he was just about to be swept by, she instinctively reached out and grabbed his robe. In her weakened condition, she was only able to hold on for an instant, but Jesus felt the tug.

"Who touched my clothes?" he asked. At that point, Peter--who had all he could handle keeping people from crushing Jesus and seeing to it that he kept making some progress toward Jairus' house--was incredulous. "You see this crowd? And yet you ask who touched you? It could have been anyone!"

But Jesus had already stopped and located the woman who had touched him. She was terribly frightened and embarrassed that she had done such a thing (the magnitude of which would only become clear to us when we learned more of her story). Nonetheless, something in the quality of Jesus' look emboldened her to come forward. Dropping down before him, she began to explain herself through her tears, as he joined her on his knees in the dusty street.

"My monthly flow of blood, after the way of women, has not ceased completely in twelve years. Twelve years! I have been unclean for that long, and the doctors can do nothing. I have no more money and my condition seemed to be getting worse instead of better. I only thought that if you would lay your hands upon me, or even if I could touch you and make contact with you in some way, I could be made well. In fact, I feel now within myself that I have been healed of this malady."

Tears glistened in Jesus' eyes as well as he sensed the depth of her confidence in him and her gratitude, not only for her healing, but simply for the attention he was giving her as she spoke. "Dear daughter of Abraham and Sarah, the faith you have shown is what has made you well. Go in peace, and be truly healed of your disease!"

Just then a disturbance arose on the periphery of the crowd, and we heard someone shout to Jairus, "Your daughter is dead. There is no need to trouble this healer further." The little girl's father nearly fainted at this news, but Jesus again caught him by both shoulders and looked straight into his eyes, "Do not be afraid, Jairus! Trust me!"

Then he asked the crowd to wait where they were. With this latest news, they had calmed down somewhat and even seemed deflated by the news about the little girl. Jesus entrusted the care of Jairus to several of us and then signaled Peter, James, and John to accompany him on to Jairus' house. This smaller team quickly covered the remaining distance but, upon their arrival, they were met with quite a scene. Family members and friends had already begun the emotional process of grieving the loss of the little girl, who was only twelve years old and quite a favorite in the village.

The sobs and wails of the ritual rang especially true in this case, and could be heard from the outskirts of town.

Jesus made his way gently but firmly though the mourners out front, and stooped to enter the little house. “Why have you started this,” he asked Jairus’ wife and her mother, “the child is not dead, but only asleep.” At this, the physician attending the child gave a disparaging snort and others actually laughed out loud at this pronouncement, according to what we later heard from James and John. But the mother’s eyes reflected a glimmer of hope and she assisted Jesus in clearing the room.

Jairus had recovered somewhat by this time and we could not keep him from joining his wife at the child’s bedside. Jesus nodded his approval and closed the door on the four of them--the mother and father, the little girl, and himself. Of course, we only know what went on inside from what Jairus said later and he was actually pretty close-mouthed about it, having been given explicit instructions from Jesus not to say much. But, apparently, after a period of silence and prayer, Jesus stroked the little girl’s hair and then took her by the hand, whispering softly, “Little girl, listen to me. Get up!”

With that she opened her eyes, focused them first on Jesus, then on her parents, and rose up gratefully into their waiting arms. Before leaving them alone as a family, Jesus reminded them that she had not eaten in several days, and that she would need food to sustain her recovery. He rarely left the practical follow-up of such an event to others, but made sure that such basics as food and drink were not left to chance. We would see that even more dramatically demonstrated before long.

CHAPTER SIX

From there we moved southwest again toward Nazareth. Jesus wanted to visit the place of his growing up, the place of his early years when Joseph was still alive and the family still intact. There was in fact some jealousy and bad feeling in Nazareth--as Jesus became better known--that he spent more time in Capernaum and some of the larger towns than he did in places like Nazareth. Some even said that he felt himself "too good for Nazareth" and that that was why he and his mother had moved to Capernaum. So Jesus was looking forward to teaching in the Nazarene synagogue again and renewing old acquaintances there, perhaps clearing up any misconceptions anyone might have concerning his feelings about his old home town. Imagine his surprise and disappointment when, contrary to the enthusiasm with which his brilliant teaching had received elsewhere, the response in Nazareth went along these lines:

"Where does he get these ideas?"

"Why does he pretend to have special wisdom?"

"I don't see him casting out demons or stilling storms here!"

"Isn't this the same one who used to work on our houses and over in Sepphoris with his father?"

"Did he not move out of Nazareth and take his mother and brothers with him, leaving only his married sisters behind?"

In other words, they found their very familiarity with him and his family history to be a stumbling block to being able to hear Jesus' message. "A prophet is never accepted in his own home town," was the way Jesus described the reaction. He tried to put the best face on it, but I could tell that he was hurt and a little depressed at their lack of response.

But it was true that healing simply did not occur with the same frequency as it had in so many other places. Oh, a few people seemed obviously better after he had prayed for them. But the vast majority, on these occasions, just rose after he had laid his hands on them and prayed, looked at him somewhat blankly as if they didn't know what to say, and wandered off. I found it, frankly, embarrassing but Jesus was too concerned about their lack of trust in God's willingness and ability to make them well to make much of it.

We left after a few days of this and it was actually many months before Jesus was even asked to pray for healing again. Instead we went from village to village in northern Palestine and he seemed to be concentrated on teaching. It may indeed have been this experience in Nazareth which prompted Jesus to begin broadening the mission. He seemed to realize now that he could not meet everyone's needs by himself--partly because of the physical limitations of being in one place at one time, and partly because he began to see that not even he would be accepted and heard equally well by everyone.

So he began to spend more time with the twelve than ever before. He even began to send them out for brief missions on their own around Galilee. He always sent them in pairs for companionship and support, and because he wanted to be as sure as possible that they had the kind of spiritual stamina and authority to handle whatever forces they might encounter along the way. Teams of two or three seemed to increase that likelihood.

They would invariably travel lightly, wearing only the clothes on their backs and perhaps carrying a walking stick. The idea was to make themselves available to whatever hospitality might be provided along the way, to stay in the homes of individuals and families, as their charity would allow, in order to make friends and build relationships which would make the hearing and acceptance of their message more likely.

These twelve were instructed not to waste much time with those from whom they received outright rejection. "Just leave immediately and shake the dust off your feet from that place as a testimony against them," Jesus told them. Their message was, of course, the same as Jesus' (which is why he spent so much time training them). It was that the reign of God was at hand, not merely something to be hoped for in the future. It was that most people were far from living into the reality of that fact, but that if they could just embrace it as true, it would turn their lives and their values completely upside down.

Like Jesus, the twelve tried to demonstrate God's sovereignty over the things of this world by bringing healing into the lives of many who were broken in body, mind, or spirit. And they would sometimes pour oil on the sick peoples' wounds, soothing them physically even as it symbolized their being anointed as kings and priests to God.

While all of the twelve were involved in these missions, not all were sent out at the same time. Several teams would fan out across the Galilee while the other six disciples would continue their instruction with Jesus. About that time, Matthew got a strange invitation to attend a birthday banquet for Herod Antipas, the son of Herod the Great, who had succeeded his father as "king." Actually the term is a bit grander than the position; he was basically tetrarch, the ruler of a rather minor political unity in Palestine.

Apparently, Herod had decided to throw himself a birthday

party since it seemed clear than no one else would. To it he summoned those who would not easily be able to say no--members of his own court, officers in his army, and civic leaders from Galilee who, more often than not, owed Herod a favor of some kind. Matthew, in his former life as a tax gatherer had certainly been in Herod's debt more than once and so received the invitation.

At first, he dismissed it with a scornful laugh. Since deciding to follow Jesus of Nazareth he no longer owed Herod anything. However, some of us encouraged him to go in order that we might learn something of the condition of John the baptizer. Within the month we had heard that John had publicly challenged Herod for having an adulterous relationship with his half-brother Philip's wife whose name was Herodias.

John had cited the Torah which states plainly, You shall not uncover the nakedness of your brother's wife; she is your brother's nakedness, and he said to Herod's face, "It is not lawful for you to have your brother's wife." Actually Herodias had hated John for years and had pleaded with Herod to have him arrested and executed for treason. Herod had always refused because he knew John to be a just and holy man, and also because he did not want to alienate John's rather considerable following.

But when John accused him of adultery practically within

earshot of the palace, he could no longer refuse her request. So, in order to defend his and his concubine's honor and his position that the relationship was not truly adulterous since Philip was only his half-brother, Herod had John arrested for sedition and imprisoned at Machaerus, east of Lake Asphaltitis on the Nabataean border--a long way from home.

At any rate, we encouraged Matthew to attend the banquet, even though he had received the invitation by an obvious oversight, to see if he could learn something concerning John's condition. We could never have anticipated what we were asking our friend to witness. Perhaps it is best to hear the story from his own lips:

"I waited until the party had been underway for a while before making my appearance. That way attention would not be called to me and the issue raised about my no longer working for the government and therefore about my right to be there. That strategy worked well and I found myself reclining at table with one of the peripheral groups, not even with Herod's main party who had arranged themselves comfortably around the central mosaic which, in Hellenistic style depicted the god Bacchus and his entourage celebrating at a similar party. As always at these events the wine flowed freely and food was much in abundance. The only thing missing was music and dancing, which situation was soon to change.

The musicians were actually hidden from our view so that, when they began playing their instruments, it was as if the music came from nowhere, and from all around us, at the same time. From one end of the room, a young woman emerged from behind a rich drapery, swaying to the music. I asked my nearest dinner companion who she was, was told that her same was Salome, and that she was actually the daughter of Herodias and Philip. I noticed that even the colleagues and supporters of Herod who were in attendance had a hard time with the blasphemy of featuring the teen-aged daughter of one's concubine and one's own brother dancing at such a gathering. But Herod Antipas seemed more captivated by her youthful beauty than by concerns of any impropriety. Herodias' look could have withered any plant in the room but he was equally oblivious to that.

She was a lovely girl and, although her rather blank expression made it clear that she had not willingly agreed to become the main attraction, the more she danced the more aroused Herod became. I heard him slur drunkenly to the man reclining next to him, 'For a night with her I would give her anything she desired.'

'Ask her,' the guest replied. And Herod summoned her when the dance was completed and the applause had died down. 'Join me in my bed,' the tetrarch leered, 'and half this kingdom will be yours instead of your mother's.'

Frightened, Salome ran from the room even as Herod roared for all the crowd to hear, 'I'll give her anything she asks for!' Herodias apparently made it clear to her daughter that she need not make any plans to replace her at Herod's side, or in his bed, and then the idea came! 'He said he'd give you anything you asked. Ask for the head of John the Baptist.' Perfect! She could keep her place at Herod's palace, get back at him for humiliating her and her daughter in public, and get rid of that loathsome traitor all in one fell swoop. So Salome, anxious to pacify her angry mother, stood at the far end of the banquet hall and clapped her hands for attention. A hush fell over the assembly at this brazen act and an expectation came for some that she would dance again. 'You said you would give me anything I want. I want the head of John the Baptist. On a plate!'

Herod cut his eyes across the room to the angry Herodias, but he knew that he had been trapped. 'Bring it!' he growled to the officer of the day. But I knew that his rage had more to do with having been bested than at any regret about John's fate. After all, this was the son of a man who had murdered most of his so-called friends and much of his family, so brutal was his fearful character. The Herods were no strangers to killing.

I bolted from the room at this point along with a number of others for whom this game had gone too far. But I could hear the soldiers readying themselves for the long ride south along the shore of the great salt sea and across it to the fort and prison where John was being held. We all had hopes that common sense would prevail, and that Herod might change his mind once he sobered up. But word finally reached us that Herod's guard had executed John personally at the prison, probably under the impression that he could win Herod's favor by so doing. A week later, the head of the fiery prophet of the desert had been placed in Salome's room. Horrified, she had it taken to her mother." Matthew shook his head in disgust and sadness as he finished the tale.

Eventually, John's disciples were able to make arrangements to recover the rest of his body--although never the head--and provide a decent burial for their teacher. While they continued to keep his name alive, they were never able to recapture the imaginations of the people in great numbers as John had done. Herod Antipas, because he was nearly as fearful of his enemies as his father had been, eventually came to believe that Jesus was John the baptizer raised from the dead, continually harassing and taunting him.

Others would sometimes say that Jesus was the fulfillment of the hope that the prophet Elijah would return just before the day of the Lord. But, for Herod, Jesus was John the Baptist, raised from the dead. An enemy he could not do away with. A prophet who would not be silent.

Nor were the disciples of the new prophet silent. All twelve of the ones Jesus had sent out on missions returned full of excitement at what they had been able to accomplish, and at how well their message was being received. Indeed most of the twelve were followed home by at least that many more who wished to learn from or be part of this new movement in Palestine.

We could see that the twelve were exhausted and finally Jesus suggested that they take a break by slipping off into the hills to rest and pray. Peter and Andrew brought the boat ashore before the morning sun rose. Jesus and the other ten climbed quietly on board to make it appear that they were setting sail for Bethsaida and the other side of the lake. Their intent was actually to land south of Gennesaret and make for the hills there.

Unfortunately they were seen word spread quickly that they were leaving the area, and a huge crowd followed along the shoreline, keeping the little vessel in sight all the way. The clamor that they made aroused even more attention and the crowd swelled to four or five thousand strong. The disciples could, of course, have changed course and headed truly for Bethsaida, but Jesus told them to turn back to the west and to make for shore.

Philip said that Jesus was somewhat conflicted in his desire to provide adequate time and space for his disciples' rest and renewal, and yet the yearning to respond to the great needs of the people he saw all around him. Finally, according to Philip, he decided that at least his disciples had him and his desire for their protection and well-being at all times whereas the crowd on the beach just appeared to be so helpless...so desperate. Just seeing the look in Jesus' eyes was enough for Andrew to push the tiller away and swing the prow of the boat toward the western shore of the lake. They landed in the midst of the crowd and this time Jesus would not even remain on the boat to teach, but moved among the people greeting them and touching them before he ever began to teach.

The rest of us joined Jesus and the twelve at just about that time and realized that he had a very responsive audience here. As always, he began with a series of parables and stories. This time there were questions from the crowd almost immediately--not challenges to his authority or theological riddles like those often posed by the scribes of the Pharisees, but genuine inquiries by people whose very lives in some instances depended on the answers. The morning passed very quickly and the sun was high overhead when it became clear that no one was going home just because it was the lunch hour.

We had left early that morning, with nothing to eat, and I was getting hungry. So were the others and, at an appropriate moment between questions, I suggested to Jesus that he dismiss the crowd so that they could find something to eat in one of the nearby villages. We could then continue the teaching into the afternoon.

"You give them something to eat."

I could not believe my ears! In front of the entire crowd, he had singled me out to provide food for some five thousand people. "Do you think we have nearly a year's wages in reserve to provide lunch for all these people?" I asked incredulously.

"How much food do you have?" he countered. "Go and see."

We scrambled on board the boat and were able to come up with only what we had packed Jesus and the twelve for lunch. I remember it distinctly--five loaves of bread and two fish! We brought this meager fare to Jesus to show him how very little it was. Instead of conceding the point, he had us ask the people to sit down in smaller groups on the green grass, family members and residents of the same villages quite naturally sitting together. All eyes were focused on Jesus as he raised the first loaf of bread toward heaven and intoned the ancient blessing: "Blessed are you, Lord our God, King of the universe, who brings forth bread from the earth." And he began to break the loaves into smaller pieces, giving them to us to distribute to those nearest us. He did the same with the fish. And so did we.

An hour later we were still carrying baskets full of bread. Only now we were gathering up the leftovers, because everyone had had enough to eat! I have no idea what happened that afternoon. I only know that, at one point, people were hungry and, at another point, people had been fed. A line from one of the prophets raced through my mind:

"On this mountain the Lord of hosts will make for all people a feast..." This passage referred to a great banquet over which the messiah would one day preside. I was not alone in making that connection. As I passed through the crowd, collecting the fragments, I saw one scribe who had actually unrolled the scroll of the prophet Isaiah and was reading the next lines to his associates there on the grass:

"It will be said on that day, See this is our God; we have waited on him, that he might save us. This is the Lord; we have waited for him; let us be glad and rejoice in his salvation." Jesus must have gotten word that such things were being said, that some were beginning to wonder if he was, after all, the "anointed one" for whom we all waited. He was invariably uncomfortable with such a facile identification, and so he abruptly ended the day's teaching session. This time he sent us off alone to Bethsaida, a fishing village at the north end of the Sea of Galilee, while he climbed a nearby mountain to be alone for a while.

It was not the best time of day for a voyage to Bethsaida.

The wind had again whipped up the waves in the shallow lake and, although it was nowhere near as frightening as our last experience on the water, we had to drop the sails and strain very hard at the oars because the wind was against us. This time, our faith must have been stronger because it was as though Jesus was right there with us, encouraging us and calming--not the storm this time--but our fears.

The whole experience was absolutely astounding to us. We still were not sure about everything that was happening. Had he really stilled the storm that first time, or was it just a coincidence? Were the loaves and fish truly multiplied, or did people simply follow Jesus' example and begin to share what they had? And which would be the greater miracle anyway? Did we really see him coming to us across the water or was his presence now that strong with us all the time? We did not know. Some of us still do not.

Finally, we gave up fighting the wind and let it blow us back to the western shore of the lake. We landed near Gennesaret and moored the boat there. Jesus was glad that we had decided not to buck the adverse weather conditions, particularly because he was again much in demand to pray for the sick. He needed our help because they were bringing gravely ill people to him now. We often had to help them carry their friends and relations in on mats, seeing them horribly emaciated and hearing their pitiful moans of pain.

As we worked our way back northward along the coast toward Capernaum, it did not seem to matter where we were--small villages, farms, or a city like Capernaum--the sick would be laid out for us to see and for him to touch. Often the sufferers would reach out to him themselves, grasping weakly for his clothing and for the four blue twisted threads which Jesus invariably wore in obedience to the law of Moses. Even getting this close to Jesus would make the sick feel better.

CHAPTER SEVEN

Word of his activities continued to make its way from the Galilee to the holy city of Jerusalem. The scribes of the Pharisees reported what they had seen and challenged their mentors to confront what they believed to be Jesus' unorthodox behavior. And, in fact, it was often to his--or our--behavior they would point. Like many common people whose lives were consumed by working to meet their basic human needs, although we observed the Torah's moral and ethical commands blamelessly, kept the major festivals and fasts associated with our people's history, and observed Shabbat in appropriate ways--the dietary laws and purification rituals were another matter.

The basic food laws of the Torah were not the problem. We ate meat only when it was well cooked and properly prepared and then only when the animal from which it came had a divided hoof and chewed the cud. We ate seafood if it had fins and scales. We ate poultry if it was fresh and clean. And, of course, we avoided mixing dairy and meat products.

Beyond that, we tried to use common sense given the limitations of time and money which our itinerant lifestyle dictated.

Jesus approved of such ways of being "a people apart" as he did by refusing to shave as the Gentiles did, keeping his head covered to show that he was a servant (a servant of God), and wearing the fringe on the corners of his garment with the blue cords to be a constant reminder of the need to remember and observe the commandments of that God. All these things we did and did happily. What we did not do--and what made Jesus furious when other people did it--was to judge other people about the scrupulosity in observing such things. For him, these were matters for personal decision. The moral laws were binding, the ceremonial laws decidedly were not.

This theological position brought him into inevitable conflict with the Pharisees, a religious movement with which otherwise Jesus found much to be in agreement. On this particular occasion the issue started out over ritual washing before meals. Elaborate ceremonies had been promulgated by the elders concerning, not just washing before meals, but exactly how and in what order the hands and face were to be washed. Like many others of the day, we simply did not participate in this rather fussy observance.

"Why do your disciples ignore the tradition and eat with

defiled hands," a Pharisee named Simon asked Jesus accusingly. The teacher slowly raised his eyes, considered his opponent for a moment, and said, "Isaiah was right when he said, 'These people draw near with their lips, while their hearts are far from me. Their worship of me is a human commandment which they have learned by rote!'"

"Are you saying that our laws are of human origin and not divine," Simon pressed, raising his voice to be heard by the crowd.

"I am saying that human traditions are more important to you than the words of the covenant!" Jesus snapped.

"Give me an example."

"All right. The fifth commandment requires you to honor your father and mother. I happen to know, Simon, that your parents are destitute, that they have asked you for help, but that you have refused, claiming that all your money is committed to tithes and offerings to the temple treasury where you spend all your time. What is more important? You ignore one of the ten words of the covenant in order observe a relatively minor discipline. And that is not the only example I could cite!"

Simon was furious, but I could see that Jesus had touched a nerve and that he had no ready reply. He fell back into the crowd just as Jesus began to address them all: "Listen, I don't care if you observe ritual purification in all its detail, or not.

It is not essential! Even the dietary laws themselves are intended to help us remember that we are a peculiar people, called by God for a special purpose. But you cannot become defiled as a person by what you eat or do not eat. It's not what goes into you that defiles you, it's what comes out! If you have ears to hear, then hear!"

We asked later what he meant by that and he said, "What you eat passes through you and out into the sewer. Even fouler is the excrement that comes from the evil intentions of the human heart--sexual promiscuity, stealing, murder, adultery, greed, corruption, lying, arrogance, foolishness. Things like that are what destroy people. You should be paying attention to them because they come from within, not from something you take in from the outside."

Shortly after that encounter, Jesus struck out on his own for a while, traveling northwest to the city of Tyre on the coast of the Great Sea. A friend had given him the use of a house where it was hoped that he would not be disturbed. However, it was becoming less and less possible for him to travel anywhere unrecognized and soon, he recounted later, a knock came at the door. Opening it, he was surprised to find himself face to face with a Syrian woman from the region. She was not, of course, a Jew and he felt the immediate discomfort he always felt in the presence of such people, an uneasiness borne of generations of isolation and suspicion between the peoples of the area.

The woman explained that her daughter was being tormented by some strange power or force quite beyond her control and that she had heard that Jesus often had success in dealing with such matters. Would he help her little girl? Although his heart was already reaching out to the suffering child, Jesus said that his first thought was that it was no wonder she was being so tormented given the undiscriminating worship of any so-called "gods" practiced by these people. How could they expect anything else? Besides, he reasoned, he had enough trouble finding time to take care of his own people, the Jews of the Judean countryside. Waving his hand to dismiss her, he found himself quoting an old maxim from his past:

"It's not fair to take food intended for the children and throw it to dogs." It surprised him that he even remembered this saying from his childhood. Joseph had never liked it and would often remind those in Nazareth who used it of the Jews' historic responsibility to care for the stranger and the sojourner as well as the descendants of Abraham and Sarah. So it was Joseph's face and voice that Jesus experienced as he heard the woman say:

"But sir, even dogs under the table are allowed to have the scraps that fall from the children's table." There was desperation in her voice and a humility which no doubt came partly from the fact that she had tried everything else, that this was her last resort, and that she knew no where else to turn.

And Jesus remembered Joseph arguing this very point in the synagogue. He even remembered the Isaian text he had cited: "And the foreigners who join themselves to the Lord, to minister to him, to love the name of the Lord, and to be his servants, all who keep the Sabbath, and do not profane it, and hold fast to my covenant--these I will bring to my holy mountain....for my house shall be called a house of prayer for all people."

Jesus did not know if this woman began to meet all of Isaiah's stipulations. But her humility came from somewhere, and her willingness to accept the lowest place for herself and her child was just the kind of thing that he did not find in the Pharisees, but found so often in common people everywhere. So he said to her, "Because you said those words you can go home happy. Your daughter's torment is over." She returned home and found it so.

After a few days, Jesus began the long trip south and east passing just north of the Sea of Galilee toward the region of the Ten Towns. Just north of Pella, the locals brought him a man who had been deaf from his birth and who therefore also spoke with great difficulty, never having heard the words himself. We were told later that Jesus refused even to pray for the man in public but took him off privately. When the man returned, he was able to hear and was speaking plainly about the fact that Jesus had put his fingers into his ears, applied some of his own saliva to the man's tongue, and--the next thing he knew--he was hearing the first word of his life, "Ephphatha!"

The Aramaic word means "Be opened" and carried the force of a command. The next words he heard were instruction to tell no one what had happened, but he was unable to keep the news to himself. Soon Jesus' reputation had spread even among the Ten Towns as far south as Philadelphia. They said, "Is there anything this man cannot do? He even makes the deaf hear, and the mute speak!" And no one could deny it.

CHAPTER EIGHT

As time went on, it became clearer and clearer that there was a convergence between Jesus' teaching and the wonderful things he was doing among the people. Space would not permit a recounting of all of these. Suffice it to say that there were many sick people who were made well, several calamities avoided, and more than once occasion where many hungry people were fed with what appeared to be very little food.

And many people became fascinated with the outward manifestations, with what Jesus often called signs, of his authority rather than the truths about God and God's reign which he was trying to convey. That was a constant frustration for Jesus, but was just fine as far as his enemies were concerned. Particularly for the Pharisees because the more they could focus on his unusual behavior and activities, the less they had to worry about trying to refute his teaching which they were at some pains to do.

Often they would challenge him to produce some kind of sign or deed precisely to cast him in the role of a "miracle worker" (of which there were many, so-called) rather than as a prophet and spokesman for God (of which there were few) or even as messiah (for whom many of us still waited). This was depressing for Jesus and he would invariably refuse to cooperate with them.

"Why do they always want signs?" he would often sigh, "They will get no signs from me today!"

Unfortunately this would often lead to his departure from a given area because so many people sought his healing presence, and it was difficult to refuse them just because there were those whose motives were less than pure. On one of these occasions, when Jesus literally had to escape by boat to avoid such entrapment by the Pharisees, we saw him begin to use the signs as ways to illustrate his teaching. They became parables in action. It all started very simply.

We had left in such haste that only one loaf of bread had found its way into our provisions. When we discovered the oversight we began joking that at least it was fully leavened and might therefore actually be enough to tide us over until we came ashore.

"Be careful not to be so accepting of the leaven of the Pharisees, or the leaven of Herod, for that matter," Jesus suddenly broke in.

"What does he mean?" James asked. "Is he scolding us for not bringing enough bread?"

"Why are you still worrying about having enough bread?" Jesus cried. "Have you forgotten seeing thousands of people fed from almost nothing? Yeast spreads its influence throughout the whole loaf invisibly. The yeast of the Pharisees is hypocrisy, and the yeast of Herod is worldliness--they do the same thing. But, I tell you, you remind me of those people Jeremiah was addressing when he said, 'Hear this, you foolish and senseless people, who have eyes, but do not see, who have ears, but do not hear! You keep listening, but you never seem to comprehend. You keep looking, but you do not see.'"

We were stung by his criticism and lapsed into an uneasy silence. We were just as glad when the time came for us to make preparations to enter the harbor at Bethsaida. Not many words were spoken as we secured the fishing boat to the dock and began unloading our supplies, such as they were. Before long, predictably, a small crowd began to assemble at the dock and among them a blind man some were bringing for Jesus to treat. He led the man carefully by the hand through the crowd all the way to the outskirts of the city where there was some peace and quiet.

They spoke softly for a while and I saw Jesus anoint the man's eyes with what appeared to be his own saliva. At first nothing seemed to happen and, in fact, this was one of the times when Jesus spent the better part of the afternoon, praying and talking with the man before any real results were seen. Gradually, with the man's full engagement and cooperation, his sight was restored. Jesus smiled and sent him on his way with the usual warning about keeping his contacts to a minimum for a while. He continued to want to avoid any notoriety for these deeds even though it seemed virtually impossible for people to keep silent after such a major event in their lives.

To us, Jesus said, "Perhaps I was too hard on you this morning. Sometimes it takes a while for those who have eyes to see, and for those who have ears to hear." And I thought about how right he was. We were like that blind man in so many ways--seeing dimly oftentimes, if seeing at all. And yet the man could see! Perhaps there was hope for us as well.

Our next journey took us straight north along the east bank of the Jordan River all the way to Caesarea-Philippi, so named because it was in the tetrarchy of Philip. One night, after we had broiled fish and eaten together around the camp fire, Jesus asked, "What are people saying about me as you travel about?"

"Well," Matthew smiled bitterly, "Herod thinks you are the Baptist, raised from death."

"And there are those who believe that you are Elijah, returning as predicted just before the day of the Lord," John said.

“Still others,” his brother added, “say that you sound a lot like Jeremiah or one of the other prophets.”

“But how about you?” Jesus said softly, still staring into the fire, “Who do you say that I am?” The silence was palpable. We all looked at each other nervously. We each had our answer to that question but, for many of us, those various expectations could be summed up in one word, one title. As was so often the case, it was Simon Peter who gave voice to our thoughts. He looked his friend directly in the eye and said clearly,

“You are the messiah.”

“Peter, don't identify me in that way! You know how differently people react to the 'coming one.' Most look for the messiah to be a king like David was, to restore the kingdom to Israel. Almost everyone believes that that will lead to all out war with Rome. Many will be killed, and for what?”

We listened carefully as he continued, “I've come to believe that that’s not what God has in mind for our salvation. Salvation doesn't mean living in a wealthy kingdom or even a land flowing with milk and honey. Salvation means acknowledging that our God is God, the only God, the only king worth serving. It means surrendering to God’s will in all things. It means offering each day to God because all days are his, and accepting everything that comes--everything!--as from his hand.

If that means suffering, so be it. If that means continued submission to the Romans, so be it. If that means the collapse of the Roman empire, so be it. If that means rejection at the hands of our own religious authorities, so be it. If it means dying, my friends, so also let it be because our God is not a God of the dead but of the living!"

Peter was furious! He grabbed Jesus by one shoulder and pushed him roughly away from the fire and toward the periphery of the camp. We could hear them arguing, but it was difficult to make out the words. Finally, Jesus pulled away and strode angrily back toward us and away from Peter. Since he was facing us, we could hear him growl through clenched teeth:

"Get behind me, Satan! I thought I had left you behind in the desert. You're not seeking God's will, Peter, but your own"

And from that night, Jesus' teaching took on a different tone. It was still focused as always on the sovereignty of God and on God's reign in the present, but there was a new emphasis on our response to that rule. He seemed to speak less of the power and glory associated with living under God's kingship, and more of the sacrifice for which that life called.

"Do you really want to follow me?" he asked the crowds (and us) the next day, "Fine, but be prepared to deny yourself and your own willfulness. Be prepared to take up burdens and risk if you follow me. Those who are so afraid of losing their own lives that they cannot take risks have already lost their lives already! But if you will give your life unreservedly to God, let it go, for my sake and for the sake of God's truth, then you'll be given a life truly worth living. Are you so sure that money and possessions and earthly kingdoms make life worthwhile? Can you buy one extra day when you are lying upon your death bed? Can you?"

At this, some of the crowd turned away in embarrassment at his passion or in shame at their own lack of conviction that what he was saying was true. But Jesus did not allow them to get away so easily. He roared at their retreating backs:

"Those of you in this faithless and sinful generation who are ashamed of me and of what I am saying, you may rest assured that I will be ashamed of you when I come in the glory of God with the holy angels!"

But his voice softened and his eyes sparkled when he turned to those of us who remained, "Don't worry, little children, some of you standing here will see, before you die, how powerful God's reign really is!"

CHAPTER NINE

It took six days for us to travel southward from Caesarea-Philippi to Nazareth. On the seventh day, which happened to be the Sabbath, Jesus once again called to himself the inner circle of disciples to accompany him to the top of Mount Tabor. Precisely what happened on the mountaintop, I do not know, but must relate it as best I can as it was told to me later in Rome by Simon Peter. In fact, I must be honest and say that there are a number of critical turning points in the life of Jesus at which I was not present but have had to rely on Peter for details. I have always found him to be a most reliable witness as, of course, have others and have no hesitancy in making his story my own.

At any rate, the four friends--Jesus, Peter, James, and John--were enjoying a cool, clear Sabbath day with a time of silence, rest, and reflection aided by a beautiful and expansive view of the lush, agricultural region of northern Palestine. The crops were nearly ready for the harvest from their rich soil and the land below the hills was alive with color. Peter had been drowsing under a tree and, as he opened his eyes, he saw the two brothers quite literally with their mouths open, staring past him toward the top of the hill.

There was Jesus standing in prayer and he seemed bathed in the brightest light Peter had ever seen! It was as though the brilliance of the noonday sun was being supplemented by a luminosity from within Jesus' own person. So deep was his communion with his "abba" in prayer that his very appearance was changed.

Never had Peter, James, and John experienced the holiness of their teacher as powerfully as in that moment. The memory of other such holy ones from their people's history washed over them: Moses coming down for the second time from Mount Sinai with the ten words of the covenant and his face veiled for the skin shone because he had been talking with God; Elijah on Mount Horeb, like Jesus here, experiencing union with God not in the wind, earthquake, or fire but in the sound of a sheer and profound silence.

A cloud moved over the face of the sun but, for Peter, it was a cloud like the one which had covered Mount Sinai. And he experienced the same truth Jesus had at his baptism in the River Jordan--this is the child of God; listen to him. The moment passed as quickly as it had come, but Peter was unwilling to let it go:

"Rabbi, let's stay and build our booths for the feast of

tabernacles right here. Three of them--one for Moses, one for Elijah, and one for you. The law...the prophets...and their fulfillment--in you, the anointed one!" He was positively babbling with excitement, fear, and joy. Slowly, Jesus opened his eyes and lowered his hands. It seemed to take a moment for him to realize exactly where he was. Then, without a word, he started down the mountain. They clambered their way down the steep path in silence for a while until James and John could contain themselves no longer:

"Jesus, do you not know what we just experienced?"

"Not exactly," he smiled, "What?"

They recounted what they had witnessed to him as best they could with all the similarities and differences each of them had experienced. And then, according to Peter, Jesus gave them a strange charge: "Do not tell anyone about this until after my death and the resurrection."

Like an increasing number of Jews, most of Jesus' disciples had been influenced heavily by the theology of the Pharisees and believed that there would be a resurrection of the dead, probably on the great day of the Lord when the messiah would come in glory. But there was a tone in Jesus' voice which made them wonder if that was the event to which he was referring. Or was this something else?

"Doesn't Elijah have to come back first, rabbi, to prepare the way for the resurrection?" John queried.

"Elijah does come first, yes, just as it is written. But remember, it is also written that I must suffer many things and be treated with contempt by everyone. And that will begin to happen soon." Jesus paused for a moment before adding, "By the way, Elijah has already come. And look what they did to him."

He said this gazing sadly off to the south toward the place where they had buried his friend, John the baptizer. Elijah.

While the four of them had been away on Mount Tabor, the rest of us had gotten ourselves into an awkward situation. Thinking that Jesus was with us, a local man had brought his son for healing. The boy was afflicted with violent seizures which the father had come to believe were caused by what he called "a mute spirit", meaning one that had no name and for which there was no explanation. Philip and Bartholomew took the boy aside with his father, commanded the spirit to depart, and anointed the youngster with oil. They had had some success with this kind of thing on one of their missions the previous spring.

This time, however, their ministrations seemed to avail nothing as the boy had another uncontrollable convulsion, stiffening and falling down, grinding his teeth and foaming at the mouth. It was horrible, and the crowd began turning angrily toward us. Some scribes of the Pharisees who were there took great delight in ridiculing Philip and Bartholomew for their lack of results, and Simon responded hotly on their behalf, ending up in a shouting match with the scribes and others in the crowd.

It was into this chaotic situation that Jesus, Peter, James, and John returned after their moving experience on the mountaintop. "What are you arguing about?" Jesus asked. Some in the crowd explained what had happened and one of the scribes added sarcastically, "They are having about as much success as you did in Nazareth!"

Jesus shook his head and said to the entire crowd, "Do none of you have faith in God? I'm not going to be around here forever, you know. In fact I'm not sure how much longer I can bear to be around you! Bring the boy to me."

As soon as they had done so and the youngster caught sight of Jesus, he again convulsed and fell onto the ground, nearly rolling into the cooking fire had he not been prevented by Peter and James.

"How long has this been going on?" Jesus asked the father.

"As long as I can remember," he answered, "And what you just saw is not unusual. He often is thrown near the fire or into the water. It's as though he wants to destroy himself before it gets any worse. Please help us if you can!"

"If I can," said Jesus in exasperation, "It's not a question of me and of my abilities. These things are possible for you if you have faith in God."

"I do have some faith, master," the man cried, "Build up the little faith I have!"

Jesus tried to move the father and his son out of ear shot, but the crowd would not leave them alone. I saw Jesus take one look at the approaching multitude and then speak very sharply to the boy. The child shrieked, was wrenched violently once again from somewhere deep within, then fell heavily into the dust where he lay still.

The crowd stopped as if one individual and I heard one woman shudder, "He's dead." But Jesus knelt on one knee beside him, took him by the hand and helped him up into the arms of his weeping father. Jesus swept the crowd hotly with his eyes. Without a word, he went into the house, slamming the door. Later we got the nerve to speak with him, "Why couldn't we do that?"

"Because you were too concerned with the crowd, with how it might all look, and with making your point with the scribes," he looked accusingly toward Simon who immediately blushed. "Besides, this kind of thing can only be dealt with after much prayer." That evening, after Jesus had retired for the night, Peter and the two brothers told us about what kind of prayer he must have been talking about. And about what they had seen on Mount Tabor.

Jesus decided the next morning that he wanted to spend some time at home so we headed north again, avoiding the western shoreline of the Sea of Galilee this time in order to elude the huge crowds we had encountered there before. Jesus seemed to want time alone with the twelve so the rest of us stayed about a half day's journey behind them. That also kept each traveling unit fairly small and made them less likely to attract attention.

We did not know exactly what Jesus was telling our companions at the time, but later learned that the theme of his teaching seemed to take a dark turn. He spoke a lot about suffering, about being betrayed by friends, even about the possibility of being killed. He also spoke more and more about the day of resurrection, leaving them with the same confusion as before.

No one really knew what had prompted this shift in emphasis except that, about the same time, he began to make it clear that he felt called to confront the authorities in Jerusalem with his messsage. We had all been dreading that possibility because we knew that it would be extremely dangerous. No one, however, dared dispute with him the wisdom or the necessity of such an encounter.

One unfortunate result of all this talk about his death was that the twelve found themselves wondering about who would be in charge if he did die. Who would the logical successor be? John the Baptist's failure to provide for an orderly transition had led to the virtual disappearance of his movement after his death. Not one of us wanted that to happen again. One evening, in his house at Capernaum, just before dinner, Jesus tried to help them with their deliberations:

"You know that whoever wants to be first must be the last of all, and the servant of all." Lifting Thaddeus' little daughter on to his knee, he said , "You need to become like this little child if you want to be first in God's eyes. Then you can be sure that whoever accepts you is not really accepting 'you' but is accepting me, and whoever accepts me is accepting the one who sent me. We must always point beyond ourselves to God!"

"But, rabbi," John blurted out, "It's going to take someone strong and bold to carry on after you're gone. Just the other day, James and I saw a man casting out demons and using your name!" He paused to smile and his brother, "But we stopped him because we knew he wasn't one of us."

"Wasn't one of us? But that's exactly what I mean! What does it mean to be 'one of us?' No one who does something good in my name will in the next breath be able to speak evil of me. Those who are not against us are for us! I tell you, you should have given that man a cool drink of water because he spoke so well in my name. Why if you'd done that," he winked at the rest of us, "you might have gotten the place of honor, after all!"

We all laughed at the embarrassment that caused the two brothers whom Jesus called "sons of thunder" because of their bombastic temperaments. But he turned serious again as he helped Thaddeus' little girl hop down off his lap and scamper out to play.

"I tell you, the people who really hear our message will be as open and accepting of the mystery of God as that little girl is. And that means that they will also be vulnerable. No one must ever take advantage of that vulnerability. If anyone does, it would be better for them if that huge millstone at the entrance to this city were hung about his neck and he were thrown into the depths of the sea!"

He continued, straining forward to make his point, "And make no mistake, my brothers and sisters, there will be judgment and there will be a final reckoning. So I warn you now, if your hand causes you to break one of the commandments, cut it off. If your foot causes you to stumble along the way, cut it off. If your eye causes you to fall short of the mark God has set for us, pluck it out and throw it away. I tell you solemnly, it is better to enter into life maimed than to enter the next life guilty by God's judgment! It would be preferable to be hurled into that stinking garbage pit of Gehenna outside the walls of Jerusalem where the fire never goes out and yet the worms never die!"

He sat back with a sigh, "Oh yes, you will be cured and

tested. But curing and testing are necessary for a true disciple of mine. Pray that you will have the strength to meet your own time of testing, and don't concern yourself with how others are meeting theirs. And, for God's sake, stop trying to be number one! Live together in peace."

CHAPTER TEN

As we began to move toward Jerusalem, we followed the Jordan River south until it emptied into Lake Asphaltitis. Continuing along the west bank of that lake, we came to the Qumran community where John the baptizer had spent so much time. The brothers there welcomed us to set up camp near the monastery (although we were not yet invited inside) and even came to hear Jesus teach when they saw the crowds begin to gather. Some Pharisees from Jerusalem engaged Jesus in a discussion about divorce and remarriage. "We are not clear about what you teach about divorce, rabbi," a man named Jacob asked. "Is it lawful or not?"

"You know the Torah well, Jacob?" Jesus smiled, anticipating the argument, "What did Moses say?"

"That when a man takes a wife and marries her, if then she finds no favor in his eyes because he has found some indecency in her, he writes her a bill of divorce and puts it in her hand and sends her out of the house."

"Sounds a bit hard-hearted to me, doesn't it to you?" Jesus replied. "I think Moses was making some concessions to the realities of life, and to the hardness of the human heart there. But if you want to know God's intention in the matter, you'll have to go back a little earlier in the Torah: 'Therefore a man leaves his father and his mother and cleaves to his wife, and they become one flesh.' So it appears to me that we are no longer talking· about two individuals here, but one whole. What therefore God has knit together in so wonderful a mystery, a man is not free to separate. If he does, he has fallen short of the standard God wills for married people."

Later, when we were invited to join the brothers of Qumran for the community meal, we asked him to elaborate further. He explained, "If sexual intercourse, which consummates a marriage, joins a man and a woman so profoundly that they can be said to be 'one flesh', then there is an integration of lives at that point which can never be truly disintegrated. Therefore, if divorce does happen after the marriage is consummated, it is almost as if any future relationship entered into--by either party--would be an adulterous one. The bond is that strong."

That afternoon the crowd returned in even greater numbers to hear him teach. Many women and children were among them this time, and I wondered if it was because of the strong stand he had taken against divorce. So many women, even some with children, were forced to live in the streets of the cities or off the land in the countryside because they had been summarily dismissed by their husbands who solemnly quoted Moses' permission as though it were a commandment.

With so many children in the crowd the noise and activity level was higher than normal in such sessions. That seemed to bother Jesus little at all, but the rest of us were a bit annoyed and concerned lest his teaching not be heard or understood clearly because of the distractions. I guess our frustration level reached its limit when, right in the midst of one of Jesus' main points, some women began making their way through the crowd, thrusting their children toward him for a blessing. We tried to stop them, but on they came, until James scolded them, "Can't you wait until the rabbi is finished teaching?"

But Jesus said, "Let the children come to me. Don't stop them for, of all the people here today, they may understand best what I am trying to say about 'abba' (which being translated is something like 'papa'). I told you before that if you do not begin to mirror the openness and acceptance of these children, you will never be able to understand what God is like!" And, one by one, he lifted the littlest children on to his lap, spoke with them for a moment and sent them off with his blessing.

We began packing for the journey to Jerusalem, but in the

midst of this activity, a young man--well dressed and well groomed, indicating that he was a man of some means--approached Jesus and knelt in front of him. “Good teacher, what must I do to have the kind of life you describe so well?”

“Why do you call me good?” Jesus smiled down at him and, as he always did to those who knelt before him, raised the young man to his feet “No one is really good but God alone. In answer to your question, you know the commandments: do not kill, do not commit adultery, do not steal, do not lie, honor your father and mother.”

“Yes, I know the commandments,” the man interrupted, “I've observed them from my earliest days!”

I could tell from the look in Jesus' eyes that he cared deeply for this young man and that he believed him. He may not have kept all the commandments as blamelessly as he would have us believe, but he really was trying to live a good life in the circumstances where he found himself. And those circumstances, Jesus surmised, were the problem.

“Perhaps you lack only one thing, my friend--freedom! Go and sell what you have...give the money to the poor...and you will have treasure in heaven. And then come, follow me!”

I was amazed. Jesus had not extended such a direct invitation to any except the twelve. Certainly he had not extended one to me, and yet I had followed him for over two years by this time. But the man's face fell and he went away.

The cost was more than he could bear. I found myself wondering how many of us would be there if we had has much to lose as that young man. Jesus seemed to verbalize my thoughts:

"It is not easy for those who are rich to put God first in their lives. It's not easy for anyone, but the rich carry so much baggage! It would be easier for that heavily-loaded camel to squeeze through the narrowest gate into the city as for a rich man to trust God with his life."

"Then who can be saved?" Matthew asked. He was still probably the wealthiest of the twelve, even though he had been generous and we had used many of his resources in our travels.

"No one will be saved by striving and striving to be perfect as that young man was doing. It is impossible to achieve the kind of salvation I'm talking about on your own. But it is possible with God's help, Matthew. Anything is possible with God's help, don't ever forget that!"

Peter spoke up, "Well, he may have been unwilling to give up everything he had and follow you, but we weren't unwilling. We have done it!"

"I know that," Jesus nodded, "And I tell you the truth, anyone who has made that kind of sacrifice of home or family or possessions for my sake and for the sake of my message will receive a hundred times more of a blessing in this life, and in the age to come, life eternal!" Then he grew deadly serious, "But don't be so sure that you rank ahead of that young man...or anyone else, Peter. Our journey is not yet complete. And many that are first now will be last then, and the last may just turn out to be first. I tell you solemnly, the hard times have not yet begun!"

Just as we were preparing actually to leave for Jerusalem, we were advised that it would be best to detour first northward to Jericho. This growing city was on the main trade route and had therefore become an important customs center. Visitors to Jerusalem often had to show proof to the occupying Roman forces that they had paid whatever duty they owed the tetrarchy of Judea. This irritated Jesus, not only because it was one more instance of Rome making life miserable for the Jews, but because he was increasingly anxious to get on with whatever awaited him in the holy city. We were amazed that he suddenly had this desire to go to Jerusalem, having studiously avoided the capital city of Judea for all these many months.

But it was clear that this was his single purpose now. It was hard for us even to keep up with him as we climbed up the dusty road from Qumran. He again wanted the twelve close by and for the same reason as before--to warn them about the impending conflict with the Jerusalem establishment. Again, the dark references to suffering and death were there, always pointing toward the mysterious day of resurrection. But when? When was all this to take place?

James and John thought it might be soon. I overheard them asking Jesus a favor, "Rabbi, we want you to do for us whatever we ask you? Will you promise to do that?"

Jesus smiled wearily, "What do you want me to do for you?"

John said, "Let my brother and me sit at your right hand when you come into your glory?"

"You have no idea what you are asking" Jesus said sharply, "can you drink of my cup and be baptized with my baptism?"

"We have done these things already!" James exclaimed, sounding like the rich young man who claimed to have kept all the commandments from his youth.

"Yes, you have." The rabbi's face softened because the two brothers had been faithful. "And you will do so again. But to sit at my right or left hand is not mine to grant. Those places are already taken."

When the other ten got wind of this conversation, they were very angry with James and John. These two were among the least popular of the twelve even though they had proven very courageous and were fiercely loyal to Jesus. There was a brazen haughtiness about them which infuriated the others. I thought Simon Peter was going to take them both on with his fists, but Jesus called us together and used this as yet another opportunity for learning.

"You are acting like the goyim," he said, spitting out a tern he rarely used. "You know how the Romans exercise their authority. They love to lord it over us. That's why we were forced to take this exra time to go to Jericho. It is not to be so among you! How many times must I tell you that whoever would be great among you must be a servant. Whoever would be first must be the slave of all. Has my life and example among you been for nothing? I have not lived my life being served, but in serving." And, he added softly, "And by giving my life, if need be, like a ransom."

Two days later, we completed our business in Jericho which turned out to be much easier than we had expected--just some useless forms to fill out and belligerent questions to answer--because we had no possessions to speak of, nor anything to declare for taxation. As we were making our way out of the city and heading up to Jerusalem, Jesus was stopped by a blind man called Bartimaeus. Matthew had known the man's father, Timaeus, through a mutual aquaintance named Zacchaeus who also lived in Jericho.

Bartimaeus cried out, "Jesus, son of David, have mercy on me!" We learned that the blind man was accustomed to sitting by the roadside at the western entrance to Jericho in order to beg from the many travelers who passed through this way. The local townspeople had little patience with him and began to berate him for causing such a disturbance. But the louder their protests became, the more insistent became Bartimaeus in his desire to be heard, "Son of David, have mercy on me!" he continued to shout.

Jesus held up his hand as a signal for us to stop, and said to Matthew, "Call him." Embarrassed and yet concerned for his friend's son, Matthew ran over to him, helped him to his feet and whispered, "Get up, and be of good cheer, he is calling you!" Bartimaeus asked Matthew to help him off with his outer garment so that he could make his way more easily to Jesus.

"What do you want me to do for you?" Jesus asked. We could hear the crowd murmuring and even a snicker or two. They knew what Bartimaeus would ask for--shekels! But this time the request was different, "Master, let me receive my sight !"

Jesus often would ask sick people to articulate their need, to name specifically what they really wanted. There were times when he would actually engage them in an extended conversation to probe a bit, to find out what their deepest need really was. Sometimes, that was not for physical healing at all, but for something even more lasting. Bartimaeus asked for sight and received it as Jesus said, "Go your way. Your trust in God has made you well." He also received something more for he followed us from that very day. Beginning with our mysterious mission to Jerusalem.

CHAPTER ELEVEN

The trip up to Jerusalem from Jericho is not an arduous one, less than twenty miles, but Jesus intended to spend the Sabbath in Bethphage on the Mount of Olives with some old friends. The holy city was even now filling with tourists and pilgrims who were there to fulfill their ancient promise to celebrate the Passover festival in Jerusalem. We did not really know anyone who lived in the city itself, but Jesus had a number of friends and supporters who lived in the nearby communities.

When the Sabbath was complete, it was to one of those villages, Bethany, that Jesus sent Simon and Judas to borrow a colt from the home of Mary and Martha. None of us were clear as to exactly why he needed a mount now that we were so close to the journey's end. After all, we had walked all the way from the Galilee, and he had set the pace most of the way! Yet, the instructions he gave were clear and suggested that some previous planning had been done of which we were unaware.

"Go over to Bethany and, just as you enter the village, you will see Mary and Martha's house. There is a young colt there which I would like you to bring me."

"What if the owners think that we are stealing it?" Judas asked.

"If they ask, just remind them that I have need of it tomorrow for a little while. We'll return it later."

The two did as Jesus had asked, and apparently ran into no difficulty because when we arose, early in the morning on the first day of the week, the colt was tethered under a fig tree near the house in which Jesus was staying. About mid-afternoon, Jesus emerged from the house with Peter and Andrew. The brothers covered the back of the rangy colt with a blanket and mantle, and Jesus swung up on its back.

We accompanied him on the descent from the Mount of Olives toward the city and, almost immediately, began to hear the shouts of Jerusalem residents as they welcomed the hundreds of pilgrims arriving for the holy week ahead.

'Blessed is he who comes in the name of the Lord... Hosanna...Blessed is she who comes in the name of the Lord...Hosanna in the highest...Blessed is the kingdom of our father David that is coming...Hosanna...Blessed are they who come in the name of the Lord." As we passed through the Kidron Valley and joined the procession streaming in through the gate of the city, we could see people spreading garments and olive branches to pave the way for the approaching pilgrims. It was a way of welcoming their fellow Jews for the Passover festival and also, as we were to learn quickly, a way to peddle their wares ranging from food items to religious adornments. It was something of a circus!

And yet there was an excitement, a sense of being "at home" with one's people even if one had never been to Jerusalem before. I thought of the ancient psalm. I was glad when they said to me, "Let us go to the house of the Lord; our feet have been standing within your gates, O Jerusalem!" And, in spite of the all the confusion, crowds, and mixed motives for being there, there was this sense of real devotion as well. We could all feel it, not least of all, Jesus.

The most touching thing however, the most moving to me, was to catch a glimpse of those who knew Jesus, or at least his reputation, and they were not an inconsiderable number even in this large crowd. When they saw him, suddenly, just like those of us who might dare to call ourselves his disciples, a light shone in their eyes. This really was the "blessed one ...coming in the name of the Lord!" Coming for Passover, yes. But a Passover such as has never been seen before or since.

It took more than an hour to move with the large crowd, through the bystanders and merchants, and actually get through the gate of the city. We left the colt tied outside the

"...when they saw him...a light shone in their eyes..."

gate and moved slowly with the crowd into the temple. Entering the city from the east we were immediately on the temple mount, but it still took almost another hour to get into the temple itself. It was as exquisite as we had expected even with the crowds, and we spent the remainder of the afternoon, silently and on our own, exploring this holiest site of our religion--from the royal porch, across the court of the gentiles, through the beautiful gate, and around Solomon's porch.

We noticed that Jesus seemed, at the same time, deeply moved by the place and yet bothered by the noisiness and irreverence of some in the crowd, and of the commercialization and even exploitation which seemed to dominate the atmosphere around those who sold animals for sacrifice and the exchangers of foreign currency for the many pilgrims. His irritation was beginning to peak when Bartholomew suggested that evening was fast approaching and that, if we intended to return the colt and stay with Mary and Martha in Bethany, the time to leave was at hand.

A good night's sleep in the home of dear friends usually soothed Jesus, but he was strangely silent during dinner and retired early that night. The next morning he was so impatient to get back to the city that we left without eating any breakfast at all. Crossing the Kidron Valley again, many of us gathered olives and whatever we could glean from the trees and shrubs to satisfy our hunger. Jesus, for some reason, made his was over to a fig tree which at this time of year had only green fruit on it. Not finding anything to his liking, he brushed aside the branches with a curse, and led us up the other side of the valley into the city once again.

This time we arrived in the temple just at the time of morning when the people were beginning to arrive in great numbers, and the commercial enterprises which had so disturbed Jesus the day before were opening for business with gusto. All of us knew why they were there--to provide a service. Travelers from all over Palestine and beyond could not transport their own animals for sacrifice over the great distances. So merchants sold pigeons and lambs and even cattle to be sacrificed for a price.

Since the whole point of the sacrificial system was to give something up for God, to deny oneself something which might otherwise be used for profit (or food) to demonstrate that God was more important, these merchants did not hesitate to add a few shekels on to the fair price in order to increase the sacrificial dimension! Similarly, the money changers were there to provide a service--exchanging foreign currency for local. Who could object to their increasing their margin of profit at the expense of wealthy pilgrims making a once in a lifetime journey to celebrate Passover in Jerusalem?

Apparently, Jesus could and did object. We had no sooner

entered the area known as the court of the gentiles than we saw Jesus charge toward the center of all this mercantile activity. He pushed a heavy wooden table backwards on to the laps of the currency dealers. and neatly stacked coins of all denominations rolled everywhere across the stone floor. He kicked over the flimsy cages of the pigeons which promptly flew off, scolding us all and leaving feathers behind. He even slipped the ropes tethering a few lambs, slapping them on their backsides causing them to bleat loudly as they dashed around in confusion, upending a few more tables and a couple of merchants.

It would have been funny (and, in fact, after the astonishment left the faces of Peter, James, and John, I'm sure I saw grins) except for the blasphemy of it all by Jerusalem standards. After all, this was the temple! The holy of holies, which contained the ark of the covenant, was here across the courtyard. The place, and perhaps the system, of sacrifice had been violated.

Jesus would have agreed. But it was not his action which had violated God's holiness; it was what the Jerusalem establishment had done to it. "Is it not written, 'My house will be a house of prayer for all the nations'?" he shouted, "You have made it a safe house for thieves!" And he stormed out of the temple with us close behind, backing out of the temple precincts to guard his back from the chief priests, the scribes, and their guards--all of whom were furious.

I would be less than honest with you, my readers, if I did not add that I then felt this incident to be less than helpful, perhaps even destructive to Jesus' acceptance by the people. On one hand, this was not unlike Jeremiah's enacted parable when he smashed the earthen flask in full sight of the people and said, "Thus says the Lord of hosts: So will I break this people and this city..." On the other hand, I simply thought this kind of action left the people confused and troubled. Certainly, it cost Jesus support and hastened the final confrontation. Maybe that was what he had in mind.

On our way back across the Kidron Valley toward the city the next day, we passed by what appeared to be the same fig tree Jesus had cursed for not bearing fruit. Peter pointed out that it had withered and Jesus said, "Just like the fig tree of Israel! I tell you, you need to trust God and God alone. If you were to command this whole temple mount to be rooted up and cast into Lake Asphaltitis, and if you had complete trust in God, that would be all that would be required to make it happen. When you ask God for something in prayer, trust that he is hearing you and answering the prayer."

Here his voice softened and I could tell he was thinking about the actions of the day before, "But when you stand praying, don't forget to forgive others if you have anything against them. For if you do not forgive, neither will the God of heaven and earth forgive you." That exchange seemed to settle him down and calm him as we once again entered the city and made our way into the temple. Jesus was walking by himself along Solomon's porch when the chief priests and some others emerged from the sacred court of priests to question him:

"By what authority are you doing these things? Who gave you the authority to do them?" I frankly thought the question was an appropriate one, given the explosive events of the day before. But Jesus countered in the dialogical fashion of a Galilean rabbi, "Let me ask you a prior question. Answer it, and I will know if you will be able to understand by what authority I speak and act. John's baptism, was it from heaven or from men?"

One of the priests was about to answer when he was silenced by his elders. The whole group huddled together to discuss the matter briefly. I knew what their dilemma was: If they gave John divine sanction, then Jesus would undoubtedly ask them why they had not only refused to follow him, but had been actively hostile to him and his followers. If they said that they believed John to have been deluded and preaching his own perverted message, they were afraid of starting a riot, since quite a crowd had gathered and among them were disciples of the baptizer.

"We don't know with any real certainty," the chief priest

said, dropping his eyes.

"Then you would never be able to understand by whose authority I do these things," Jesus said, shaking his head sadly. As he walked away, most of the crowd followed, for it was clear that he had bested the religious authorities once again.

CHAPTER TWELVE

He moved from there to the wall of the city, sat down, and began to teach those who had followed him out of the temple, using his favorite method--story telling. "Once there was a farmer who planted a vineyard. He put a hedge around it to protect it (like these walls which protect the city), he dug out a place for the wine press so that it would be convenient right where the grapes would grow, and he built a tower in the midst of the vineyard (as high as the temple mount). But then he found that he had to go to a far country on other business so he rented the vineyard to tenant farmers."

"When the time came for the grapes to ripen, he sent a servant to the tenants for a sample of the fruit his vineyard had produced. But they did not believe that the servant had come from the owner. They thought he was an imposter so they beat him up and sent him away. A second time the owner sent an emissary to retrieve some fruit from his own vineyard and he received the same treatment. Yet a third time he tried, this time sending written documentation that the servant was authorized to represent the owner. But the tenants claimed that it was a forgery and abused the servant so badly that he died."

"Finally, the owner took drastic action, 'I'll send my son to them! Surely he has the proper credentials for them.' But by this time, the tenant farmers had become hardened and possessive of the vineyard. Their only thought was, 'This is the heir. One day all this will belong to him and we will be out. Unless...' And, right outside the vineyard hedge, they killed him as well! Now, what do you think the owner will do to those scoundrels?"

We had little doubt as to the answer to that question, and Jesus confirmed it for us, "He will get rid of them and give the vineyard away to others." The context in which Jesus told this parable and the physical setting, sitting on top of the walled city of Jerusalem, left no doubt in anyone's mind as to its meaning--especially when we thought back to the psalmist and to the prophets who so often used the vineyard as a symbol for Israel:

"You have brought a vine out of Egypt; you cast out the nations and planted it. You prepared the ground for it; it took root and filled the land...Why have you broken down its walls, so that all who pass by pluck off its grapes? Turn now, O God of hosts! Look down from heaven, behold and tend this vine, preserve what your right hand has planted."

Less clear were his other analogies. As we moved outside the city walls, we walked by an old, abandoned stone quarry. The rock had long since been mined out, leaving only a heap of stones surrounding a huge boulder which had only been left because it had a fault in it. "Have you never read in the psalms," he asked, "The stone which the builders rejected has become the cornerstone? This is the Lord's doing; it is marvelous in our eyes?" Only later did we learn for what purpose the abandoned stone quarry and the spoiled rock were being used. And the analogy became clear.

Meanwhile, we learned that the chief priests and the temple guard had approached Caiaphas, who was high priest that year, with the request that he call for the arrest of Jesus on the grounds that he had desecrated and spoken ill of the temple and its ritual. His violent actions earlier in the week, his besting of them in debate, and his transparent story suggesting God's judgment on Israel had led them to conclude that Jesus was a dangerous reformer who needed to be dealt with firmly before it was too late. Caiaphas was inclined to agree with them, but was also aware of Jesus' popularity with the masses and was therefore reluctant to alienate them by taking action too swiftly.

Instead he suggested that a coalition be formed and that some of the brightest of the Pharisees, Sadducees, and perhaps an official or two from the king's court be dispatched to engage Jesus in public debate, hopefully to discredit him once and for all. The first such confrontation involved a supposed argument between a Pharisee and a representative of the government as to the legality of religious leaders paying taxes to Rome. A small delegation, who had ostensibly reached an impasse in their discussion and debate on the matter, approached Jesus with feigned deference,

"Rabbi, we know that you are a truthful man and that you are not afraid to take a position even when it offends people in high places if you believe it is consistent with God's will. We have a question for you--is it lawful for us to pay taxes to the emporer and his government or not?"

Jesus immediately saw through their little ruse and knew that this was no philosophical debate they were bringing to him. This was a test. And one which did not have an easy solution. It had been argued for decades without clear resolution. It was also a trap. If he said Yes, the zealots would call him a lackey of Rome and the authorities might even use it as an argument to raise some local taxes. If he said No, he would be cast in the role of political revolutionary who was a danger to the state and who should probably be arrested.

He gazed at them pensively for a few moments before answering them and then said, "So you are putting me to the test! Does someone have a denarius I could see for a moment?" Someone produced the large coin and tossed it to Jesus who turned it over, studying it carefully as though he had never seen one before.

"Whose image is this?" he asked with a small smile, "Who authorized its minting and stands behind its value?"

"The emperor's, of course," sneered Herod's courtier.

"Then it seems appropriate to give back to emperor the things of the empire," and with that, Jesus tossed the coin to him. "Just don't forget to give back to God what belongs to God!"

It was a brilliant answer. The crowd laughed and clapped their hands at the befuddled looks on the faces of Pharisee and court official alike. Now, it was the Sadducees' turn. An even more important and longstanding argument within Judaism than the lawfulness of paying taxes had to do with whether there would, or would not, be an ultimate resurrection of the dead.

One strand of the tradition (represented in our day by the Sadducees) argued that eternal life meant life lived in relationship and harmony with the Eternal One, with all the strength and direction which that could provide for one's life here on earth. According to this tradition, life as we know it ends with physical death and any extension of one's personality beyond that was lived through one's children and their children. Hence, the emphasis on the Jewish family and on the importance of producing heirs.

The other extreme (represented by the Pharisees) believed that there would be a general resurrection of all those who had died. This would occur on the last, great day of the Lord when the messiah would come and establish the kingdom for Israel. Personal holiness and faithfulness was emphasized by this group, for it was on those qualities that ultimate judgment would be based. Even within this tradition there were variations--some believed that only the just would be awakened from the sleep of death, others that all would be raised with some being rewarded by eternal life with God and others being consigned to eternal death or punishment without God.

It was common knowledge that Jesus embraced this latter perspective and was, in that sense, a Pharisee. So the Sadducees presented him with one of their classic arguments against the logic of a personal resurrection. And to do so, they cited the ancient and widespread custom of levirate marriage which Moses had embraced. That is, it was the duty of a brother-in-law to raise up a male descendent for his deceased brother, should that situation occur, and to perpetuate his name and inheritance. The Sadducees were strong advocates of this tradition given their emphasis on everlasting life coming through the perpetuation of the family name.

But what if death was not the end? What if, at some point

in the future, the dead brother was raised? To whose home would the woman belong, the brother-in-law (whose wife she was now) or the brother (whose wife she had been)? It was this question that the Sadducees posed to Jesus, compounding its complexity by the hyperbole of suggesting that this could occur more than once in the same family should the brother-in-law follow his brother in death.

Jesus' face showed the exasperation evident in his response, "You're confused about this because you know neither the scriptures nor the power of God. First of all, when Moses stood before the burning bush of Sinai, our God identified himself as the God of Abraham, Isaac, and Jacob. He is the God of the living not the dead, and those patriarchs are alive to this day. Besides, in the resurrection, there will be a new order. The old will pass away, and our existence then will be as different from our existence now as the angels are from us. Relationships like marriage will not be necessary then, for we will all be united in God. Once again, you are dead wrong!"

And once again, by invoking the image of Moses and the burning bush, Jesus had prevailed in rabbinical dialogue by pushing beyond the technicalities of the Torah to core values and concepts from the earliest strata of our tradition. This actually pleased the scribes of the Pharisees, who loved this kind of textual dispute, and so they decided to push him one step further, "Since you have answered so well, rabbi, but have set one passage from scripture over against another, perhaps you could tell us which commandment is greatest of all? What is the highest law?"

This was an age-old question. And Jesus began his answer with the classic definition of monotheism, belief in the one God, the ancient shema, "Hear, O Israel: The Lord our God is one Lord!" But they had asked for a commandment so Jesus continued with a slight variation of the first of the ten words Moses had brought down from Mount Sinai, "You shall so love the Lord your God--with all your heart, soul, mind, and strength--that you put nothing before him in your life." Everyone nodded, surprised at his orthodox response, but Jesus continued, "And if you want to know the second most important commandment, it is this, 'You shall love your neighbor as you love yourself. There is no greater commandment than these.'"

Again, Jesus' adversaries were stunned by the comprehensiveness of his answer. In two statements, he had summed up the decalogue--the first four of which have to do with our duty toward God, and the last six of which have to do with how we love our neighbors. Finally, one of the scribes said, "You have answered well. The oneness of God and the importance of loving God and other people is more important than all the burnt offerings and sacrifices we could ever make at the temple altar."

The Sadducees would have had a hard time accepting that completely, but Caiaphas' delegation had the good sense to call this off before it went any further, and they drifted away in silence. Jesus momentarily halted the scribe who had last spoken and said to him quietly, "You are not far from the kingdom of God."

Although Jesus had impressed some of the scribes with his knowledge of the scriptures and his thoughtful answers to thorny theological questions, most still did not trust him and looked for opportunities to trip him up. After one of the hours of prayer, at about three o'clock in the afternoon, Jesus sat with a small crowd of worshippers, teaching from the scriptures. Apparently he had decided to turn the tables on the scribes and to test just how far they were willing to go with their strict interpretation of the text.

"So, given what I've said," he began, "Is it correct to call the messiah 'son of David'?" They all nodded enthusiastically for they thought that he had demonstrated that point well from the law and the prophets.

"Then how can David himself write in the psalms, 'The Lord says to my lord: Sit at my right hand, till I make your enemies your footstool'?"

Although Jesus was convinced that the psalm cited was a royal psalm, written for a coronation, and that the second use of the word "lord" referred to one of the kings of Israel, the scribes had long considered it a prediction of the coming messiah. It was widely quoted as such and yet, if that was the case and if it was written by David, then it had him referring to a descendent in a way unheard of at the time--The Lord said to my lord.

In short, all of this could not be true and yet the scribes went on quoting it glibly, seemingly oblivious to the difficulties with the text. That is, until Jesus challenged them on it! They could hardly resolve the conflict without either denying David's authorship or denying that it really did refer to a coming messiah. They were prepared to do neither so they remained silent--much to the delight of the crowds.

Seizing the opportunity, Jesus spoke directly to the crowd, "Beware of these scribes who are so sure that they have all the truth that they go about in costly robes, are greeted solicitously in the marketplace, have the best seats in the synagogues--and at lavish feasts. They will eat the last morsel out of a widow's pantry, and consider it their due for intoning an interminable table blessing! They will be judged more harshly by God than you."

Then Jesus turned his attention toward the temple treasury and to those who lined up to make monetary offerings: "Look at the rich who put denarius after denarius into the box, never missing it at all because of their great wealth. What they give back to God is less than they would toss a servant for a job well done."

About that time, an old woman--obviously a widow by her clothing and abject poverty--approached the treasury and dropped in what sounded like a lepton, a copper coin of little value. The timing could not have been more appropriate and I saw tears well up in Jesus' eyes as he said, "I tell you solemnly, that woman has contributed more this day to God's temple than all the rest combined. They tithed, all right. But she gave everything she had. And, in doing so, she gave her life to God!"

CHAPTER THIRTEEN

Leaving the temple precincts and heading back across the Kidron Valley, we paused to view again from afar the beauty of the temple pinnacle against the vesper sky. Judas was standing next to Jesus and was overcome with the sight of it all, "Just look, rabbi, at the stonework and at the size of those buildings! How did they do it?"

"Do you marvel at that, Judas?" Jesus replied, "I tell you, one day, one day soon--like all such buildings made with hands--they will all be reduced to rubble."

Well, you could hear the gasps from everyone! On one level, we knew that such monuments do not last forever. There were enough ruined palaces and formerly fine homes demolished to convince us of that. Even the temple had been destroyed before. But most of us liked to believe the tradition which pointed to this temple standing forever. Or standing at least until the messiah would come and restore the kingdom to Israel. So, after we arrived back on the Mount of Olives, I overheard the inner circle of the twelve along with, on this occasion, Andrew ask Jesus, "When will this be? And how will we know that it is beginning to happen? Will there be a warning this time?"

Jesus closed his eyes and began to disclose things to them which he had never discussed before, "First of all, you need to be on guard lest you be led astray by people who will either claim actually to be messiahs or will claim to speak in my name. Some people will believe them. You will hear about wars or possible wars and some will see these as signs of the end of all things. Don't listen to them and do not let all this frighten you. These are not the signs of the end. There have always been wars and there always will be. There have always been natural disasters and there always will be. These things are as inevitable as the distresses associated with child birth. Don't even pay attention to such things. Pay attention to yourselves and to the quality of your lives together as my disciples. For soon they will hand you over to councils and you will be beaten even in synagogues and you will be brought before gentile rulers on my account. But this will be your opportunity to testify before them. The message of our God's grace and power must reach all nations before it is too late.

So, when they do put you on trial, don't worry about what to say. Instead speak the words given you by the holy spirit in that hour. It will be a time of trial--for brother will deliver brother to death, and the father his child, and children will have their own parents put to death so evil will the days become. But those who endure it all to the end will find their salvation.

Now as to the destruction of the temple, I see it happening again. I don't know exactly when it will happen, but it could be soon. When you see pagan practices in the temple again, then let those who live near Jerusalem flee to the mountains, and let them do so immediately not even pausing to gather their possessions or clothing. Pity the poor women who are pregnant or have little ones in those days, and pray that all this may not happen in winter. For the affliction will seem as great as anything this world has ever seen or is likely to see. If God did not shorten this time, no human being would be rescued. But, for the sake of his chosen ones, he will shorten the time. This too will pass.

So again, if people say to you, 'Here is the messiah' or 'There he is', do not believe them. False messiahs and false prophets will arise and will do signs and wonders which will tempt even you to fall away. But do not be deceived by them; I have told you all this to forewarn you. Now after all this has occurred, it will be as though the sun and moon are darkened, and the stars are falling from the heavens! The whole universe will be shaken. Then, and only then, will the son of man appear with the clouds and great glory. And his messengers will gather the elect from the four corners of the earth, from the ends of earth to the ends of heaven.

Let the fig tree teach you its lesson: when you see its leaves you know that summer is near. So too, when you begin to see these things taking place, you will know that he is near. I tell you solemnly, this generation will not pass away before all these things begin to happen. Heaven and earth will pass away someday, but what I have taught you will never pass away.

However, do not try to predict exactly when all this will occur. No one knows--not the angels in heaven, not me. Only God knows. Therefore you must be constantly vigilant like a doorkeeper when the master of the house is on a journey. He must remain on watch lest the master return--in the evening, or at midnight, or at cockcrow, or later in the morning--and find him asleep instead of on the job. Like him, you must live as though your master could return at any moment. Stay awake!"

Peter told me of these words years later, and of how confused they had all been at what he said. The events, as Jesus described them, seemed almost outside of time. Did he mean that the Romans were about to destroy our temple? And would that precede the persecutions he describes? Who was this mysterious "son of man?" Who are "the elect", "his chosen ones?" They didn't really know, according to Peter.

Some of us still don't. So we watch...and wait.

Chapter Fourteen

The following Tuesday we were having dinner in the home of a Pharisee named Simon with whom Jesus had been in disputes in the past. This young man had unexpectedly contracted the dreaded skin disease known to us as leprosy. He had been shunned by his former friends and was re-introduced to Jesus by Mary and Martha who lived near him in Bethany. Jesus had prayed for his healing and the disease seemed to have been stopped in its early stages.

Simon had overheard the chief priests and scribes plotting to arrest Jesus and charge him with some capital offense for which he might be put to death. Jesus' revolutionary approach to Judaism, his growing following, and the most recent confrontations in the temple had become intolerable for the Jerusalem establishment. I have always believed that part of it had to do with the different styles and approaches of the rabbinical synagogue-centered Judaism of the north (which was Jesus' tradition) and the priestly temple-centered Judaism of Jerusalem.

As Galileans, we were accustomed to not having all the answers. We were farmers and fishermen. Our religious tradition included raising hard questions for debate and dialogue, arguing with the texts even of the law and the prophets in order to find an even deeper truth. Our rabbis were famous for it. But these chief priests and scribes in Jerusalem seemed to see everything in black and white, yes or no. They were committed to a sacrificial and a ritual system which said, "If you have done this, then you must atone by offering this or that sacrifice or by following this or that particular procedure." Jesus was likely to respond, "Why? And what does all this have to do with the ever-present love and power of God?"

At any rate, the leadership of this Jerusalem establishment had already decided to arrest and try Jesus for sedition and, if possible, blasphemy. The only question was when and where to seize him. According to Simon, some wanted to do it immediately, even before Passover; others were suggesting waiting until the crowds began to dissipate after the Feast of Unleavened Bread on Thursday evening. The tension was thick in the room as we discussed all this over dinner, and I noticed that Jesus had barely touched his meal.

As we pushed back from the table and continued to weigh our options, I noticed a young woman approaching with a beautiful alabaster jar. We were all jumpy and I saw John move toward her as she drew nearer to Jesus. The rabbi sensed the movement, turned to watch the woman, and held up his hand for John to let her approach him. She seemed to be in a kind of dreamy, detached state of devotion as she slowly raised the alabaster jar, broke it open, and poured the precious contents--a few drops of very expensive perfumed oil--into Jesus' long, dark hair. His eyes never left hers as she smoothed his hair with her hands and brought the oil down both cheeks into his beard.

This was too much for Simon the Zealot and Judas who were concerned about two things--the woman's proximity to Jesus and her extravagant expression of love for him demonstrated by this anointing with costly oil, imported no doubt from India. They seized her arms and Judas said, "What are you doing? Why waste this nard when it could have been sold for a year's wage and the money given to the poor?"

Jesus said, "Let her alone. Take your hands off her! She has done a beautiful thing for me. Perhaps, if what we've heard tonight is true, she has begun the preparations for my burial. And what is this sudden concern for the poor, Judas? They've always been around us and they always will be. Whenever you like, you can start doing good to them. But you will not always have me."

Then he turned to the woman and said, "Thank you. I tell

you, whenever my story is told, what you have done for me will be remembered." At that point, Judas pushed through those of us who were gathered around and bolted angrily though the doors, slamming them behind him. We found out later where he had gone that night...and what he had done.

When Thursday arrived, and the lambs were being slaughtered in the temple in preparation for hundreds of Seder meals, Philip asked Jesus where he and the twelve--as a kind of family--would eat their Passover meal together. Jesus selected Peter and Andrew, sending them off with the following instructions:

"I have already made arrangements for this, but we have to be careful if we are to avoid the chief priests and the others. At noon, be at the Damascus Gate to the city. You will meet a man carrying ajar of water. Follow him and, when he enters a house, go in and say to the owner, 'The rabbi wants to know where his guest room is for the Seder.' The room he will take you to is upstairs, safe and protected. You may begin making preparations immediately for tonight."

Later, Peter told me that they had followed his instructions to the letter and found everything just as he had described it. Then they went to work, setting things up for the meal. And there was much work to do. They had been given red wine and matzah by Mary and Martha, but had to purchase herbs, salt, eggs, apples, cinnamon, and almonds from local merchants. Peter procured those items while Andrew negotiated with the owner of the household to split the cost of a lamb with his family. The table, pitcher, plates and cups came with the room and needed only to be arranged and adorned with flowers and candles for all things to be in readiness. The table setting would simple, but nothing essential would be omitted. After all, this was Passover in Jerusalem!

And the events of this Passover night were dramatic and important. I have had to rely, once again, primarily on Peter's account for most of this, although I observed some of it from afar. As the sun set, Jesus and the twelve were gathered in the upper room. They had come singly or in pairs throughout the afternoon to avoid detection. Peter said that the tone of the meal, the atmosphere--usually celebrative on Passover night, especially for pilgrims in Jerusalem--was somber and tension-filled. There was very little conversation except for the Passover ritual with Jesus taking the role of the head of the household and various members of the twelve taking the other parts. But the silence was shattered when, just as he was preparing to dip the matzah into the green herb mix, Jesus said, "One of you, eating at this very table with me, is going to betray me." He said these words with anguish in his voice and as though they had been ripped from his throat by the poignancy of this intimate gathering soon to be fractured by betrayal.

The twelve were incredulous at his words, and began asking for further details as to who the betrayer might be. But Jesus would only say, "It is one of the twelve, one who is dipping bread in this dish with me." And he sighed deeply, "I am prepared for the necessity of dying, but pity that man who betrays me. It would have been better if that man had never been born."

Moments later he changed the words of the familiar Passover ritual. Instead of the usual words spoken at the breaking of the bread, he took the matzah in his hands and, after saying the blessing, he broke it and, as he did so, he said, "This is my body."

It was so dramatic! And so clear. His body was to be broken like the bread. He really was going to die. Or at least that is what he was anticipating. And later, over the cup of wine, after the blessing, he said, "This is my blood of the covenant which is poured out for many. I tell you the truth, I shall not drink again of the fruit of the vine until I drink it new in the kingdom of God."

Peter sensed that this meant that Jesus' death was close at hand. They drank wine at every meal, so this might mean that Jesus would be dead before the next day. Or did he mean he would begin a fast from wine? Or was he speaking only of the Passover cup of wine, which would give him another year? Peter's senses were reeling, and he barely remembered the conclusion of the meal and the singing of the final psalms. The normally festive tone of the Seder was non-existent. And rather than hearing the words of the psalms celebrating Israel's freedom from slavery in Egypt, Peter could only pick up a few isolated lines, like cries in the night:

"The snares of death encompassed me; the pangs of Sheol laid hold on me...Precious in the sight of the Lord is the death of his saints...They surrounded me, surrounded me on every side..."

They left quickly and this time all together as though the need for secrecy was somehow past. Thirteen men, Jesus and Peter in the lead, making their way out of the city and across the Kidron valley again to the Mount of Olives. As they strode quickly, Jesus noticed that Judas was no longer with them and said, to no one in particular, "You will all fall away. But I don't suppose I should be surprised. It is even written in the book of the prophet Zechariah, 'I will strike the shepherd, and the sheep will be scattered.' But, one day, after the resurrection, I will see you all in Galilee!" Peter protested, "Even if they do all fall away, master, I will not!" But Jesus stopped abruptly in the middle of the road and looked squarely at Peter with a mix of sadness and anger, "I tell you solemnly, Peter, on this very night, before the cock crows twice, you will deny me not once, but three times!"

"Never," shouted Peter, "I may die with you, but I will

"...Jesus pitched forward...lying prostrate in penitential prayer..."

never deny you." And the others chimed in as well, giving similar expressions of loyalty.

Jesus just turned wearily and began the climb up to the Mount of Olives.

Partway up the mountain, Jesus led them into an olive grove called Gethsemane. It was a place to which he had come several times during the last week to reflect and pray. It was for that that he had come once again and this time he asked Peter, James, and John to go with him. It was clear to Peter that his friend was in great distress and he felt strangely relieved when Jesus confessed that openly, "Peter I, am frightened to death and so sad that all this is happening! Please stay with me and keep watch."

Moving deeper into the grove of olive trees, Jesus pitched forward on his face, lying prostrate with his face on the ground in the ancient posture for penitential and supplicatory prayer. James, who had followed Jesus, heard him pray audibly, "Abba, all things are possible for you. Please remove this cup from my lips!"

And James knew that he was begging God to spare him from what lay ahead. It was a painful thing for James to watch his master in such turmoil. He didn't understand any of this. But one thing was clear--there was little or nothing he could do about it. This journey, whatever it was, Jesus had to walk alone.

The difficult week, the long day, the emotional turmoil of this evening all had taken their toll on the three disciples. As Jesus' time of prayer dragged on into the early morning hours, the quiet of Gethsemane finally lulled them to sleep. Jesus woke Peter once with a stern rebuke, addressing him not by the familiar nickname--Peter, the rock--which he had given him, but by his old name, "Simon, are you asleep? Could you not watch one hour? Wake up and at least pray for yourself that you may be able to stan in the time of trial. I tell you, though the spirit may be willing to do what God asks of us, the flesh is weak."

He went off to pray again, and Peter tried to as well. But the late night prevailed and again he fell asleep. When next he was awakened by Jesus, he became aware that--at some point during that long night--Jesus' prayer must have changed from "Take this cup from me" to "Nevertheless, let your will, not mine, be done." For although Jesus was still deeply distressed, there was new strength in his voice. He said, "Still sleeping? Enough, the hour has come. I have been betrayed into their hands." Peter wondered just how he knew that, and then the sound reached his ears--the rustling of the undergrowth.

And Jesus said coldly, "The traitor is here."

I don't really know if Jesus knew who that traitor was going to turn out to be. He simply heard the approaching crowd and knew that they had been led there by someone. When Jesus, Peter, James, and John had peeled off into Gethsemane on their way back up the Mount of Olives from Jerusalem, the other eight (minus Judas) from the supper joined us in Bethany. They told us what had transpired at the supper--about the likelihood of a traitor in our midst, and about Jesus' increasing conviction that he was about to die--and they told us that he had gone off to pray with the others in Gethsemane.

My only thought was to be near him as well, so I ran down the hill toward Gethsemane without even bothering to throw on my outer garment which I had removed in preparation for sleep. Halfway there, I saw a crowd moving up from the city. There were soldiers with swords and clubs and were being led, it seemed to me, by the chief priests of the temple, the scribes of the Pharisees, and some of the older leaders of the Jerusalem establishment.

Taking care to keep myself out of sight, I arrived at the little clearing where Jesus and his disciples were conversing just as the armed crowd burst onto the scene. From out of the crowd stepped Judas Iscariot, one of our own number, who greeted Jesus with the traditional kiss. Looking back on it, I suppose it is less than surprising that Judas should have been the one to betray Jesus in this way. Like Simon the Zealot, Judas had come to us from a revolutionary background and perspective. He hated the Romans and wanted desperately to see them expelled forcibly from the country. He constantly pushed Jesus to be more vocal on the political situation, and became increasingly disillusioned when Jesus refused.

Some have felt that Judas may have been trying to force Jesus' hand by provoking a final confrontation. Others believe that his disillusionment had turned into genuine antipathy and his hatred of the Romans began to extend to anyone, like Jesus, whom Judas believed to be complicit by their silence on the foreign occupation. I don't know what motivated my brother to do what he did, and I was as close to the moment of betrayal as anyone save Peter, James, and John. I do know that, from my place behind an olive tree, I watched Judas take Jesus by the shoulders, look him squarely in the eyes, kiss him on both cheeks, and say, "Master."

Then, pandemonium! The temple guards seized Jesus and threw him to the ground in order to tie his hands behind his back. Peter and the two brothers leaped to his defense, but were themselves beaten badly and subdued by the angry crowd. At one point, Peter broke free, drew the short, heavy-bladed sword he always carried, and swung it at the nearest adversary, mangling his forehead and ripping off his right ear.

The man screamed through the blood and Jesus struggled to his feet, while still being restrained, and shouted, "Stop this! Have you come out against me like you would a common thief, with swords and clubs? I've been among you, unprotected, every day in the temple teaching. You did not seize me then! But, let the scripture be fulfilled."

I took this last to be yet another reference to the dark theme which had begun to dominate our master's teaching in the last months. He had come to believe that somehow suffering was necessary--not to be sought out or glorified for its own sake, but inevitable in the service of God. And that somehow it was through the doorway of suffering that the redemption could come. This was utterly contrary to what most of us looked for in the messiah and it was one reason that many of us continued to wrestle with whether or not Jesus was the one for whom we had all been waiting.

Meanwhile, the violence in Gethsemane was continuing. Peter was unconscious and, before they suffered a similar fate, James and John escaped through the trees. I remained hidden at some distance, until they began to lead a battered and bruised Jesus back down the hill toward the city. I tried to follow quietly, but was soon discovered by two of the guards. I knew of their brutality and, when one of them stripped me, I left the piece of cloth hanging in his hand as I ran away naked with the sound of their jeers ringing in my ears. That night I was stripped, not only of my clothing, but of any illusion that I was willing to die for Jesus. Clearly, I was not. And I never saw his face again.

Peter, on the other hand, was not about to give up so easily.

He regained consciousness just as the last of the crowd had left the olive grove to head back into the city. Lying still for a moment to clear his head and to make sure no one saw him move, he decided to follow, at a safe distance, just in case there was an opening and Jesus gave some sign of wanting to escape. Peter actually knew some of the guards and, when they had delivered Jesus to the high priest, they let him join them for a time in the courtyard, provided he promised not to make trouble. They had no brief against Peter as long as his master--who had somehow aroused the ire of their employers--was safely under arrest. From his place near an open fire, Peter was able to hear the discussions inside.

Apparently the chief priests had summoned a number of witnesses to testify against Jesus. They seemed to be vying against one another to see who could come up with the most serious charge against Jesus, perhaps to receive the reward which had been offered for such damaging testimony. It seemed obvious to Peter that a number of those witnesses had never heard Jesus teach at all, and were making their stories up out of whole cloth.

Others reported positions stated by Jesus containing just enough of the truth to sound familiar. For example, instead of citing Jesus as having said, concerning the temple, "One day like all other buildings made with hands this will be reduced to ruins," they quoted him as saying, "I will destroy this temple make with hands." But even with these false witnesses, their testimony did not agree and the case was not very convincing. So the high priest that year, whose name was Caiaphas, turned directly to Jesus and asked, "What do you have to say for yourself? Do these men tell the truth or not?" Peter could not hear Jesus reply, and assumed he had refused to answer.

"Are you the messiah?" Caiaphas continued, "Answer me! Are you the son of the Blessed One?" Peter held his breath and closed his eyes. What would Jesus answer to this question? He remembered the time, over a year ago now, when Jesus had asked them, "Who do you say that I am?" And Peter had replied, "You are the messiah!" How Jesus had avoided it! He seemed to feel that all titles were inadequate and limiting, even ancient and revered ones like "Messiah." But so much had happened since those days. How would Jesus respond now to the high priest's questions, "Are you the messiah? Are you the son of the Blessed One?"

"I am," Peter heard Jesus say firmly. "And you will see the son of man seated on the right hand of Power, and coming with the clouds of heaven!" "Blasphemy!" screamed Caiaphas. "We don't even need these witnesses. You have heard it from his own lips. What is your decision?" This one-sided gathering of Jesus' enemies needed no further prompting. "He deserves to die," they said with one voice.

Peter's stomach convulsed in fear and the bile rose in his throat. "It's over," he thought, "It's really happening. All our hopes and dreams...And he's not even trying to defend himself or escape. Where is his power now? Maybe I don't even know this man anymore!"

He stumbled blindly out of the courtyard as the guards moved in to seize Jesus again. His last glimpse of the man he had loved so deeply, of the man he had tried to hard to understand, was of him being spit upon by the scribes and elders and being bludgeoned by the guards. Blood mingled with sweat began to mat Jesus' hair. And Peter knew that there was nothing more he could do. The death penalty had been called for.

Making his way to a lower courtyard in a daze, Peter sat slowly down on a low wall and gazed despondently into the dying embers of a cooking fire until a crowing rooster heralded the impending dawn. One of the high priest's kitchen servants approached him tentatively, "You were one of those with Jesus of Nazareth, weren't you?"

Peter never took his eyes off the fire, "Woman, I don't know who you mean."

She went back to her work and Peter sat there a long time until the embers grew cold and the pre-dawn air began to chill his bones. As he made his way slowly back to the forecourt, the servant caught sight of him again and said to some standing by, "This man is one of them." Peter shook his head and tried to ignore the small gathering of servants, beggars, and thieves who were out this early in the morning. But one of them sneered, "You must at least know him. After all, you are from the Galilee." All the sorrow, anger, and fear in Peter's heart framed his bitter reply, "May God damn me if know the man of whom you speak! I swear that I do not!"

And, as the sun peeked above the rocky Judean hills, the cock crowed. For the second time.

And Peter remembered.

CHAPTER FIFTEEN

As a subject people, the Jews of Palestine were not allowed to carry out the death penalty on their own. They could only recommend such action to the Roman government which was normally more than happy to comply with their wishes, provided the trial had been carried out in accordance with Jewish law for which they had great respect. So, after an early morning conference with the hastily assembled Sanhedrin to ratify the sentence in Jesus' case, a small delegation including Joseph of Arimathea who was a respected member of the council seen to be neutral in the case of Jesus, took the prisoner to the palace of the Roman governor whose name was Pontius Pilate. It is from Joseph that we later learned what transpired next.

Pilate was aware that the delegation was seeking the death penalty, and so he asked for the privilege of interrogating Jesus himself, "So you call yourself 'the king of the Jews?'"

"Those are your words," Jesus replied with a controlled voice.

The chief priests immediately began their accusations and recounting what Jesus had confessed before Caiaphas. Pilate was confused, “Aren’t you going to respond to any of these charges?” Jesus stared straight ahead and said nothing.

“I don’t want to get involved in these internal Jewish squabbles over theology,” Pilate said in exasperation, “As long as he doesn't cause trouble for Rome--and therefore for me--I don't care if he’s the messiah or not! You've had kings before. Listen, you know that it is my custom to release a prisoner of your choice during your Passover time. I mean, the whole festival is about freedom, isn’t it? What if I were to release 'the king of the Jews’ this Passover ? Wouldn’t that please your people? I’ve heard this man is very popular.”

“We’d rather have you release the man called Barrabas, “one of the chief priests replied. “But he’s a rebel and a common murderer!” Pilate exclaimed. The chief priest drew himself up, “He’s a patriot!”

“Then what am I going to do with this man whom some call messiah?”

“Crucify him,” one of the elders hissed.

“Why?” Pilate asked desperately, “What evil has he really done?”

“He has been convicted and sentenced according to our laws with testimony out of his own mouth which I heard,” shouted the chief priest, “Crucify him!”

"All right," sighed Pilate wearily, "I don't want any trouble with you people." And, summoning two soldiers, he snapped, "Take him away and follow the usual procedures. There are two crucifixions scheduled for today anyway. Add him to the list." With that, Pilate turned on his heel and left without another word.

"The usual procedures" in these matters involved torture and flogging designed partly to satisfy the brutal passions of those who desired vengeance against the convicted criminals, and partly to weaken physically those who were to be crucified so that they would spend less time on the cross before dying. We were never sure if this was what passed for Roman compassion or was in the service of Roman efficiency. At any rate, after beating him with a leather whip the tips of which contained bits of metal, the soldiers led Jesus out and summoned their whole battalion to join in the fun.

When the word spread that he had been called "King of the Jews," the soldiers dressed him up like a mock king, with a cast-off cloak of faded purple and a crown woven hastily out of branches and thorns. "Hail to the king of the Jews!" They shouted this scornfully and immediately knocked him to his knees with a blow to the head from a short, wooden baton. They spat on him while he struggled to his feet, hands still bound behind him as they had been for hours. Then two of them dragged Jesus over to a stone bench which looked a bit like a throne. Sitting him down upon it, they stood on either side like courtiers and commanded their raucous comrades to kneel down and pay him homage.

Joseph of Arimathea arrived about this time and observing the action for only a few moments, could stand no more of it. "That's enough," he shouted to the soldiers, "For God's sake, get it over with!" They sneered at this lone member of the Jewish council whose orders, of course, they did not have to take. But he was a wealthy man, used to being obeyed, and his voice seemed to have a sobering effect on the soldiers. They stood Jesus up and stripped him of the filthy cloak, revealing to Joseph for the first time the horrible raw wounds left by the lash. Lifting the heavy crossbeam to his shoulders, they untied his hands and strapped his wrists to it before beginning to kick and push him toward the city gate.

He would have to be taken outside the walls of Jerusalem for crucifixion and this meant winding through the early morning streets. Merchants were beginning to stir in the marketplace and lingering pilgrims were beginning to make their way home after the festival. Seeing one led away for crucifixion was not an uncommon sight at least for the Jerusalem residents. It happened with chilling regularity, and the macabre "parade" through the city served as a reminder of just how Rome dealt with those who dared challenge her authority.

Jesus received the same reactions from the populace as others before him had. Some joined the soldiers in spitting on the condemned one and jeering at him, assuming that he must be a thief or a murderer and, in any case, wanting to look good in the eyes of their Roman overlords. Some were sympathetic and even tried in various ways to help. One of these was a Cyrenean who helped Jesus up once after he had fallen under the weight of the cross beam. The solders transferred the wooden beam on to his dark shoulders when it became clear that Jesus was too weak to carry it, and they began to tire of the slow progress through the streets.

But most of those out and about on this Friday morning just ignored the whole scene, averting their eyes and pretending to give new attention to their early chores rather than to view, once again, this troubling spectacle. The small party of soldiers, observers, and the one to be crucified arrived at their destination.

It was an old stone quarry just outside the city walls. It had been worked for years until most of the usable stone had been removed. There was remaining a huge boulder which unfortunately had a deep fault running through it and was therefore not worth the effort. Someone had remarked that it looked rather like a human skull and so it became known as Golgotha, the place of the skull. The Romans could think of no better place for executions to take place, and so that same stone, rejected by the builders, became doubly the place of the skull.

One of the standing orders was for the soldiers to offer those condemned to crucifixion a drug made of wine and myrrh to dull the excruciating pain of being nailed to the cross, and the slow death by suffocation which would follow. But Jesus turned his head when it was offered and refused to drink it. So, they pushed him roughly down on his back, stretched his arms above his head and along the cross beam, and hammered the heavy spikes through his wrists into the dark wood.

Jesus screamed twice and then lost consciousness, briefly and mercifully, while they stripped him of his remaining clothes (which they would later steal), lifted the crossbeam with its bleeding prisoner on to the stationary upright, and fastened his feet in the same way. Only the rough-hewn crotch piece kept the weight of his body from tearing away from the nails. Three women who had often been with us, Mary of Migdal, Mary the mother of James, and Salome, were the only ones of our number who witnessed all this, and they wept openly for him in the morning sun. It was only nine o'clock in the morning.

Each of the crosses bore an inscription to let all who passed by know precisely what the charge had been. This was seen as a deterrent to any of the rabble who might actually see it and pay attention. As Pilate had said, there were two other crucifixions that morning and they had already taken place. Each of their inscriptions read, "Thief" while Jesus' said contemptuously "The King of the Jews."

About that time, a crowd began to gather. Joseph recognized some of them as witnesses at the trial, still hurling their accusations, "You who claim to be powerful enough to destroy the temple and rebuild it in three days, save yourself and come down from that cross."

"He claimed to save others," another in the crowd, a priest, sneered, "He can't even save himself" Another of the chief priests taunted, "If you are the messiah, as you and your inscription claim, come down from the cross that we may see and believe you."

Incredibly, even the two thieves, dying alongside Jesus, cursed him in their final agony.

The day itself never seemed fully to have dawned. For, although the sun moved on toward its noonday peak, it was shrouded by overcast skies for much of the day. The three women stayed near the foot of the cross long after the other bystanders had drifted away. It was not a pretty sight for them to see. As Jesus weakened physically from loss of blood and from all that his body had suffered, his head began to fall on to his chest and his entire body sagged forward. This, of course, was precisely what crucifixion intended for this cut off his breathing and made it difficult for him to fill his lungs with air. This was how the death penalty was supposed to work.

Periodically, this slow suffocation would become intolerable and Jesus would try to pull himself into a more upright position, and gasp for air. But this sent spasms of agony from his nailed hands and feet throughout his entire body. He could not stand that for long, and so would finally slump forward again, gasping in pain and for breath. The women knew that this could not go on forever, yet the minutes seemed like hours and the hours days. And still he suffered.

By three in the afternoon, Jesus' lungs were beginning to fill with fluid. But he inched his body once more up on the cross so that he could catch a breath. This time he made a sound. The women crept nearer and heard him cry out, "Eloi, Eloi, lema sabachthani." Or at least that is what they later decided he must have said, "My God, my God, why have you forsaken me?" A cry of dereliction from the psalms.

At first they thought the initial word was "Elijah," that great prophet who was to return in liberation just before the last, great day of the Lord. This excited the women! Perhaps there was yet a chance. Perhaps Elijah would indeed come to save him--to save all of them! Mary ran to bring a vinegar-soaked sponge to quench his thirst and revive him. But, before she could return, Jesus cried out one last time. And died.

Some said, at that very moment, the veil in the temple which closed off the holy of holies from the people was torn completely in two. That suggested to them that this moment had fundamentally altered the relationship between God and his people. But the women who stood nearest the cross saw only the death of their rabbi. And they heard the commanding officer, who was required to stay until the bitter end, utter a grudging word of respect for the way Jesus had died, "Truly, this man was a son of God!"

Later that afternoon, Joseph of Arimathea wandered despondently back to the place of the skull. He had not felt good about the so-called trial, nor about his own silence. He had himself heard Jesus preach about the reign and sovereignty of God and had heard nothing other than what he too believed. And, while the accusations about destroying the temple were serious, the witnesses' stories were too confused to be compelling. Blasphemy was another matter, but he had only Caiaphas' word for that, having never heard Jesus blaspheme with his own ears. He had been just about to ask some further questions when Caiaphas put it to a vote and then selected him to be one of the delegation to take Jesus before Pilate. He knew that there they had to present a united front. So he was silent.

Joseph stood for a long time staring at the dead body of

Jesus, still nailed to the cross. This was the first time he had been part of carrying out the death penalty. And he did not feel good about that either. Why this man? Why him? The only thing he had ever heard Jesus teach was that God was sovereign and that we were not, that God cared for us and that therefore we should care for one another. Was that so revolutionary? Did he have to die for that?

Joseph shook his head and turned toward the governor's headquarters. Not many Jews would have had access to Pilate late on a Friday afternoon, but Pilate knew Joseph of Arimathea--and he respected him. "What do you want, Joseph?" he asked as soon as the Jew had been ushered into his presence.

"1 would like to be given custody of the body of that man you sentenced to the cross earlier today. Jesus of Nazareth."

"The one they call 'king of the Jews?'" Pilate laughed, "Whatever for?"

"I'd like to provide him with a decent burial. I'm not sure we did the right thing here."

"1 tried to get him off," Pilate bristled.

"1 know you did," Joseph nodded, "And I'm ashamed of myself for not speaking up."

"Forget it. What's the death of one man?" Pilate waved his hand. "I've killed hundreds. He's not dead yet, is he?"

"Yes, he was on the cross for about six hours. And your

soldiers had their way with him even before that."

"He'd better be grateful, "Pilate grinned, "I've seen men last for days if they were in good shape and the weather was mild."

"May I have the body or not?" Joseph snapped.

"Yes, take it," the governor replied, "Maybe that will salve your conscience concerning this man!"

Joseph thanked the governor and headed back quickly toward Golgotha, making one stop along the way at his own home to enlist the help of several of his trusted servants. It was now moving on toward late afternoon and the sabbath observance was fast approaching. If he was to finish his work today, he would have to hurry. As Joseph and his servants began their grisly task of taking Jesus' body down from the cross, they were joined by two women. Joseph recognized Mary from Migdal as one who had been close to Jesus, but did not know her companion that day.

"May we help?" Mary asked.

"You may indeed," breathed a grateful Joseph, "Bring along that linen shroud and maybe later you can help us prepare the body for burial."

When the body was removed, they washed it and Joseph led them all to a rolling stone tomb not far from there which belonged to his family. Such tombs were very costly and consisted of a large chamber where the body was anointed with oils and spices, then wrapped carefully in its burial cloth. The body was laid on the stone floor of this central room and those who prepared the body stood down in a trench which was some four feet deep so that they could more easily accomplish their work.

When the preparations were completed, the dressed body would be removed to one of six or seven tombs which radiated, like spokes from a hub, off the central chamber. Normally, the bodies would remain in these smaller rooms for two or three years before being removed to be replaced by other bodies. The bones which remained were then taken to a family grave site, and the deceased was finally "gathered to his ancestors."

Joseph and the two women were not far into the preparation of Jesus' body when it became clear that sunset was fast approaching and that they would have to leave Jesus' body in the central chamber, finishing their work only when the Sabbath was past.

"There is no difficulty," Joseph assured the women, "The rolling stone will seal the tomb and we can return on the first day of the week."

"It would be an honor for us to complete this task for you," Mary said softly, "There is no reason for you to return if only you will send your servants, early Sunday morning, to roll away the stone and seal it again when our work is done."

Sensing that they genuinely wanted to do this last good deed for their rabbi, and not at all troubled by being relieved of this unpleasant work, Joseph agreed. They parted without a word after seeing the huge rock moved into place, securing the entrance to the tomb.

CHAPTER SIXTEEN

Early Sunday morning, after spending a strangely somber and empty Sabbath day on which they invited Salome to accompany them, the two Marys and their friend set out to complete the final preparations for Jesus' burial. Salome had been eager to help and had brought extra spices with which to anoint him. The sun had barely risen when they approached the tomb.

Nowhere were the servants who had agreed to meet them to be found, and they began to wonder just how they could ever roll the large stone away by themselves. And who could they trust to ask for help? But, as they approached the door of the tomb they saw that it had already been rolled back a bit. Assuming that the servants had arrived early and would return later to finish, the three women moved from the early morning sunlight into the darkness of the tomb. What they saw and heard there so stunned them that they fled from the site, trembling with equal measures of fear and joy!

Hours later, Mary--still dazed and reeling from the

experience--related it to Peter, whose haggard look and reddened eyes spoke volumes of the anguish he had suffered over the last days. Mary sketched in the background quickly and then, her voice quivering, whispered:

"Peter, we went into the tomb, expecting to find his body. Instead we saw a young man, sitting off to the right," she closed her eyes to visualize again the scene, "He was dressed in a white robe, and I was frightened! I leaped back toward the door, but he said, 'Don't be afraid! I know you are looking for Jesus of Nazareth who was crucified. He is not here. He has been raised from death! Look, here's the place where you laid him. Now go tell his disciples, and especially Peter, that he is going on ahead of you to Galilee--just as he told you. You'll see him there.'"

"And, Peter," Mary grabbed his arm, her eyes glistening, "I believe him!"

EPILOGUE

Things were chaotic after that, for a while. In fact, since I had run away that night in the garden I stayed well away from Peter and the rest of Jesus' friends for quite some time. Later, I heard that a number of his followers--Mary of Migdal, Cleopas and his wife, and the remaining eleven of his closest companions--had actually experienced Jesus as being alive again! This was often in the context of a shared meal of some kind.

They came to believe that they were to continue his ministry of teaching and healing, that they were to baptize others as Jesus himself had been baptized, and that nothing they would ever face could ever finally deter them from this mission. After a while, these personal experiences of Jesus seem to have occurred less and less, and they began to understand that he was now somehow "with God" in a new way and would only be present with them spiritually, yet powerfully nonetheless.

I moved in with my cousin Barnabas in Jerusalem and, years later, was introduced by him to a man named Saul who had originally been a vocal opponent of this new "sect" of Jesus' followers. In fact, he had actively arrested and assisted in the execution of some of my friends. This, until Saul himself had a similar spiritual experience with Jesus while traveling to Damascus.

So powerful was this encounter that Saul himself sought baptism, became a "follower of the Way," changing his name to Paul. He was later introduced by my cousin to Peter and James and the others in Jerusalem all of whom were amazed that this supposed persecutor of Jesus' companions now sought to be one of them. After that, Barnabas and I moved to Antioch to build up the community in that city and Paul was invited to join us.

Barnabas and Paul became inseparable for a while,

traveling together, and raising money to help out their friends in Jerusalem when they experienced a severe famine. I accompanied them for a while, but gradually decided that I wanted to return to Jerusalem and consult with Peter about writing down the story of Jesus before it all faded from our memories. Paul, who never got along well with Peter anyway, did not think that was a good idea and we all had a falling out which took years to heal.

When it finally did, I accompanied Paul to Rome and, I like to think, played some role in reconciling him to Peter. In any case, he seemed no longer to object when I began meeting with Peter editing my notes which eventually took shape in this little book.

As I suggested in the beginning, this is a different kind of book. Not so much a biography as a kind of testimony. I just want people to know what an extraordinary figure this Jesus of Nazareth was. I know that he may well be forgotten someday.

But not by me.

ABOUT THE AUTHOR

The Rt. Rev. C. Christopher Epting is a bishop in the Episcopal Church. After serving as a priest in both urban and rural communities for sixteen years, he was elected the Bishop of Iowa in 1988. He was the episcopal pastor of this community for more than a decade before being called by the Presiding Bishop of the Episcopal Church to represent the church as its Ecumenical and Interfaith representative.

From 2001 through almost another ten years he travelled widely, meeting with faith leaders around the world to build new bridges of understanding and cooperation. He was instrumental in crafting an agreement that led to full communion between the Episcopal Church and the Evangelical Lutheran Church in America.

It was during a sabbatical at St. George's College in Jerusalem that he began writing the book that was to become JOHN MARK.